AND A WHITE MOON BEAMS

Published by Sarum Publishing.

With thanks to James McCarraher.

ISBN: 9798749190861

Printed in Great Britain

AND A WHITE MOON BEAMS

L J Collins

Laurence (Larry) J Collins served as a soldier before becoming a teacher. He

then worked as an actor for a number of years before lecturing and writing part-time while serving as a volunteer officer. He wrote numerous articles and published books on management and cadet history. In 2000 he received an MBE.

Publications:
THEATRE AT WAR 1914-18.
CADETS –The impact of war on the Cadet Movement.
CADETS AND THE WAR 1939-45.
MANAGING CADET VOLUNTEERS.
A GUIDE TO MANAGING UNIFORMED VOLUNTEERS.

Fiction, short stories:
A TALKING ARROW.
TALES FROM THE RANGE.

Plays:
THE LETTER.
THE FINAL CURTAIN.

CONTENTS

The story alternates between the coast of south-east England and the battlefields of Belgium and France.

CHAPTER ONE

Gordon Hemmings pulls up and locks the car in the detached garage; ensuring the car is put away has become routine since the war began. According to the police, any invading enemy will make straight for the bigger houses and in particular those with a car parked in the drive. None have so far been stolen, but 'you never know' warns his wife.

The couple enter through the stylish Georgian front porch with its ornate filigree fanlight; coats are hung in the hallway and they make for the dining room. Gordon collects the prepared supper from the top of the polished chestnut sideboard; the dinner plates are set at opposite ends of the mahogany dining table.

'Where's James?' enquires Moira.

'I don't know. He could have cycled to Manston to see the aircraft.'

'That boy's obsessed with flying. You ought to stop him going.'

'You know I can't do that. He's not a child anymore. He's old enough to be in the military. Flying is new, it's exciting. He'll be annoyed he missed seeing the zeppelin. You know very well he wants to join up – go into the Royal Flying Corps.'

‘Well he can’t. I need him here. You need him at the factory. Thank God he’s in a restricted occupation. Anyway, working in a munitions factory is a valuable job. They won’t take our son,’ snaps Moira and then hesitatingly adds … ‘Will they?’

‘No they won’t take him, but …well, not at the moment’

‘But … Well what! You’re not encouraging him to enlist are you?’

‘No. No. Of course not’, snapped Gordon.

Gordon’s mind turns again to the problem of the increasing demand for additional munitions output. Although this is secondary to the news he has recently read in the press. As a result of the proposed introduction of conscription there will inevitably be a further demand for accommodation. This was headlines in the local paper. The editor underlined the fact that ‘some of the occupants of large country houses are voluntarily moving to smaller lodgings and renting out their homes for the duration’. Gordon decides not to convey this news to his wife; she’ll find out soon enough when she reads the newspaper. He knows her real worry. She doesn’t want to lose her house, even temporarily, but more than that she’s terrified of losing her son, so is Gordon but he believes the latter is a possibility.

‘Do you think the band will be playing on the promenade this Bank Holiday? It’s not the same without them,’ inquires Moira in an attempt to breach the silence.

‘I doubt it. They’re too busy escorting troops off to the Front and onto the ships at Folkestone.’

‘I’m told they play them off but not when they come back.’

‘Hardly surprising … most of those returning are on stretchers!’

‘I don’t want to see our James on a stretcher …’

‘There’s little chance of that happening while he works with me. You go to bed dear. I’ll wait for James.’

Moira rises wearily from the table. ‘You will make sure he gets something to eat, won’t you?’

‘I will. Good night dear.’

The diminutive Moira closes the door quietly and is heard wearily trudging her way up the stairs to their bedroom.

Gordon doesn’t dwell at this time on his wife’s unease, or of the possibility of their son having to leave home. He occupies himself with his work and scans through the pages of accounts in preparation for a forthcoming meeting. He is pleased with the work his son is doing in the accounts department. The boy has proved to be a quick learner and his methods are thorough, another reason why he too doesn't want to lose him, but Gordon is a realist, and expects the worse.

The crunch of bicycle tyres on the pebbled drive heralds James's approach. The bike is stored in the garage.

A young 19 year-old athletic looking James enters the kitchen. His dark hair is ruffled by the wind and his pale face flushed due to the hurried pedalling along the four miles from the airfield. James stands 5' 9", some seven inches taller than his mother and one inch shorter than his father. He shares the personality of both; his desire for risk taking is an echo of his father's personality, but behind this youthful spirit there is a quietness of thought underpinned by a social diffidence - traits inherited from his mother.

'Hello dad, you still up, where's, mum?'

'She's gone to bed.'

'I see you're checking my sums, all OK I hope?'

'Yes, you've passed muster.'

‘Glad to hear it. By the way, where did you and mum go this evening? No point in going to the beach now the Navy’s put it out of bounds. There’s barbed wire everywhere.’

‘We had an interesting encounter, well not exactly an encounter … we saw a bloody great zeppelin overhead.’

‘Really’, exclaims James. ‘Did you know that zeppelins can turn off their engines and drift silently along at 11,000 feet?’ James always becomes animated when talking about anything to do with aircraft.

‘Yes, of course I know. We had first-hand experience.’

‘Did it drop any incendiaries? Did the ships fire back? Wish I’d seen it.’

‘No need to get excited. Nothing happened. It was probably on its way back from an attack on London or maybe the pilot was reconnoitring our defences. Anyway, where were you? Don’t tell me … Manston airdrome.’

‘Yes, I watched the planes being scrambled. I expect they were chasing that zeppelin you saw.’

‘Well, it got away. I think it was out of range of the artillery and probably climbed too high for our aircraft.’

James slumps into an armchair in a corner of the room. The look on his face doesn't belie his feelings and he emits a long sigh. He is at an age when all, or practically all, of his ex-school friends have enlisted in the Army or the Royal Navy. Those who are not in the military full-time are serving part-time in a uniformed capacity. He feels that he is on the periphery and that he ought to be more fully involved in the war effort, despite the fact that both his mother and his father keep reminding him that he is doing a vital job. As if to underline the point his father has a copy of Lord Kitchener's letter framed and hung on the wall in his office, in which the Field-Marshal and Secretary of State for War, spells out the importance of munitions workers, it reads '*They ... are doing their duty for their King and Country, equally with those who have joined the Army for active service ...*'

Vital contribution or not, James is bored with doing accounts and managing the stores. He can't help noticing that as the war goes on some of the girls in the factory are expressing their doubts – although not to his face – as to his willingness to serve his country in its hour of need. They may assume that he is getting out of military service because he's the son of the general manager. Some 'tut-tut' as he walks by, others turn away. How much longer, he wonders, might it be before he is presented with a white feather?

Gordon Hemmings is not unaware of his son's dilemma. He is torn between encouraging him to stay at home for his

mother's sake and thus protecting him from the vagaries of war, and from encouraging him to do his duty elsewhere. Being a bit of a gambler and a chancer in his day as a merchant seaman, he is used to facing danger; he understands how James must be feeling. At nineteen the boy doesn't want to be out-of-step with his peers. As it is he has little to do with his pals, most of them are serving abroad while James remains working long hours at the gunpowder factory. Fortunately there is no argument with the authorities, who constantly remind people via the newspapers and radio, of the importance and strategic value of such occupations. If he was down the mines or in ship building, where most of the workforce are male, it would be different. But ninety per cent of the munitions workers are female, the remaining males being either ineligible for military service due to their age or medical unfitness: thus they are exonerated from criticism.
'I see the authorities are asking for more volunteers to be special constables. What do you think, dad?'

'That's alright for those who work regular hours. They can guarantee to be on duty when asked. We, as you well know, have to work shifts. This means you would be unavailable much of the time, therefore, you wouldn't be of much use – would you!'

'I suppose not,' retorts James, dejectedly.

'Your mum's asked cook to leave you some supper in the kitchen, there's ham and cheese sandwiches.'

The grandfather clock in the hall chimes eleven when Gordon finally closes the audit book and moves towards the door.

'Good night dad'. James rises and moves to the dining table.

'Night son, don't be late. We'll be leaving at 5.30 tomorrow morning.'

James toys with his supper. He is not in the mood to eat. His thoughts are preoccupied with flying. He tries to imagine what it would be like to climb into a cockpit and take off in search of the Hun. Like most young men of his age, and despite working in munitions, he has a rather romantic view of the war.

One of the advantages of an early start is that they arrive at the factory prior to the shift change.

They avoid seeing many of the girls hanging about outside indulging in a smoke-break before starting work; they do not see him arriving in his dad's car. He feels self-conscious arriving with the boss. Most of the girls couldn't care less that he may appear to be chaperoned. They are more impressed by the fact that he actually turns up in a car. The girls either walk from the town having travelled by train, or cycle to the factory. Although nineteen years of age, James still feels rather embarrassed when stared at by the opposite sex.

CHAPTER TWO

Beryl Cooper is calling for her daughter to get up. 'Susan, your breakfast is getting cold. If I wait any longer, I'll miss the train'. With that she grabs her holdall and slams the door on her way out.

Her mood is one of uncertainty and apprehension. Husband Harry is coming to the end of his basic army training. It will be nice to have him home on leave, but then he'll be off to France or Belgium and the Front: and then what?

The local train is crowded with workers travelling from Margate and other towns along the coast of north-east Kent. It is normally a reasonably pleasant journey. It is just two stops before Beryl is to alight. This morning there is a slight drizzle and the sun is still below the horizon, hence the carriage windows are shut and the air is rank with the smell of cigarette smoke and perspiring bodies; it is a relief to get off the train at Faversham and walk the last couple of miles to the gunpowder factory. The whiff of sea ozone emanating from the mud flats of Oare Creek act as a refreshing inhalant.

Workers, mainly girls, are entering the gates in pairs, some chatting others still coming to terms with the early morning start. Beryl, once a housemaid now a better-off munitioneer, hears her cousin calling her.

‘Morning Beryl’ shouts Dolly Smith. ‘How’s your Harry? Has he been home yet for his final leave?’

‘Don’t say final, Dolly. It’s his last leave before he goes abroad. I bloody hope it ain’t his final one!’

‘You know what I mean. Where’s he going, France, Belgium, Salonika, where?’

‘Don’t know. Doubt if he does … the Kent boys are in France.’

‘Oh! Good. I mean our George can show him the ropes, he’s an old soldier now – been there six months.’

‘What did he say it’s like?’

‘He doesn’t say much. They censor his letters. Anyway, you know he ain’t much of a talker, never mind a letter writer. Still I miss him. Young Charlie pines for him but I won’t let him see me crying for his dad. Now he’s turned thirteen he’s trying to be a man, bless him. I’ll see you on the weekend.

I've got a letter for George; it might be quicker to give it to your Harry to deliver.'

'Come over Saturday morning and have a cup of tea.'

'Right, see you then.'

The cousins part and make their separate ways to their specific work areas.

Working in a munitions factory is hazardous. Dolly appears to have the less dangerous job operating the large lathe, although she is always complaining about the grit from the grinding machine getting into her eyes. The grit inflames her eyelids. The soreness has to be relieved, so every two days or so she goes to the first-aid centre for cleansing treatment.

Beryl walks to the other end of the factory and another department. Beryl has a different problem. She is a member of a group of women known as 'canaries' on account of their yellow tinged skin. This is a result of continual exposure to the sulphurous TNT. The women look as though they are suffering from a form of yellow jaundice, not a pleasant experience. But it is war time and the hundreds of thousands of 'Munitionettes' are proud to be doing their bit.

The camaraderie in the factory is palpable amongst the workers, despite the grumblings about pay and conditions.

Whenever they complain, the boss, Gordon Hemmings, reminds them of the hardship and dangers their husbands, sons or boyfriends are enduring at the Front in France, Belgium and elsewhere. It is hard to contradict this argument. But as Beryl has pointed out many times, ‘How does he know? He’s never spent time there and his boy works here, at home!’ This phrase is uttered with feelings of begrudging resentment. The other girls nod in agreement.

‘You do realise,’ says Dolly Smith addressing the girls in her section while putting on her authoritative steward type voice, and quoting from the local newspaper, ‘that over 80% of the weaponry and explosives expended by the British Army are manufactured by its female workforce.’ The facts are emphasised by adding, ‘Namely us! And, despite the bloody awful factory conditions, we are paid less than any of our male co-workers.’ This is a point she has made forcefully, on numerous occasions to the boss. A sort of emancipation is in evidence as wages are beginning to rise. Nevertheless managers such as Gordon Hemmings regard the girls as temporary labour, destined to be employed for the duration only.

To add insult to injury the factory workers have to pay for meals, there are no subsidies, no bonuses. The pay for filling shells is only twenty-five shillings a week for a female employee; considerably less than that paid to a man. Now there is talk of some form of industrial action. The more strident and vocal protestors such as Dolly are adamant that all the workers should take action.

'I think we should go slow, work to rule,' demands Dolly. 'We do you silly mare,' retorts one of the workers 'only ... it's their rule not ours ... besides it against the law to strike!'

It is difficult to know what the women can do. Prior to the war most of the girls didn't have a job or if they did, it would probably have been in service; for many this meant living and working miles from home for even less money. 'I know some people think we munition workers are onto a good thing, making a shed load of money. Well, we ain't and you know it.' There is a collective nod of agreement.

'Come on, come on we got a bloody war to fight ... get on with your work,' barks the corpulent foreman and irascible, Mr Woods.

The girls are proud of the diminutive Dolly; she's five foot and two inches tall and slimly built. She's known ironically as 'Dynamite Dolly'. Despite her lack of inches she has the courage to stand up to anyone, including Mr Woods, who can be awkwardly officious. On one occasion he attempted to record the amount of time some of the female workers spent visiting the toilets. His excuse was that they were slowing down production. In retaliation she timed a couple of the male workers and presented the results to Mr Woods: there was no significant difference.

The banging of hammers on metal resounds around the building, although it is slightly quieter in Beryl's work bay as she and her immediate work mates are separated from other departments owing to the toxicity of the TNT. She wonders to herself how long it will take for her jaundiced looking skin to return to something approaching normal. It has been some time since Harry has seen her and she is convinced that she has turned a deeper shade of yellow; 'would this upset him, put him off,' she thinks. Only time will tell.

At six p.m. the hooter sounds and Beryl's ten hour shift has come to an end. The munition workers hurry out of the factory gates. Although the dark evening air is a relief from the stifling and noisy atmosphere of the work place, it is depressing to go to work in the dark and emerge at the end of the long day still in the night of a winter's day.

The train rattles on through the now desolate resorts of Whitstable and Herne Bay, stopping on its way to the Isle of Thanet. Beryl gets off before it reaches Margate and makes her way to the edge of town in the hope that her daughter, Susan, has got home before her. If she has, tea will be ready; otherwise it will be up to her to prepare the evening meal. She'll be pleased to put her feet up. She's been standing for nearly ten hours and her ankles are beginning to swell. At 35 years of age she is young enough to cope but what the long term effect will be who knows?

Susan is one of the reasons why Beryl sought employment in the munitions industry; it enabled her to work nearer to home and family. Her daughter, like many of her contemporaries, was initially seduced by the excitement of war. Things changed of course once she, along with everyone else, realised it would not be over in the prophesied six months. Susan had already acquired first-aid knowledge as a cadet with the St John Ambulance Brigade and it was a logical progression for her to train to be a nurse. In truth she also liked the idea of donning a uniform, and what is more romantic for a seventeen year old girl than the uniform of a nurse. Beryl was impressed by her daughter's action and was also pleased to be seen contributing directly to the war effort.

Susan works in one of the recently set-up voluntary military hospitals in Canterbury. A fortuitous posting in that it means she too can live at home and, more importantly, occasionally see her dad while he was undertaking the first part of his basic military training at the local barracks. That was before he went off to train at a camp on Salisbury Plain.

'Hello mum, is all OK? Good day at the office?' calls Susan with a touch of friendly sarcasm.

‘Oh, Yeah until some bright spark decided to spill some of the highly dangerous toxic material. Stupid mare! We had to evacuate our part of the building. Still, can’t complain, it gave us time for a smoke break.’

‘No real complaints, then?’

‘No, except that fat supervising bugger, Mr ‘Groucho’ Woods, said we still have to produce our quota.’

The factory foreman can best be described as a round man whose girth is wider than his shoulder. In his fifties he is too old for the military. His general demeanour – and his moustache – is reminiscent of a music-hall sergeant-major.

‘What about you?’

Like her mum she too is looking forward to seeing her dad again, but she is concerned. Working in the hospital has opened her eyes to the effects of war. On seeing her first case of blistered and amputated limbs she went weak at the knees and passed-out. ‘I hope dad doesn’t end up like that,’ she remarked to her mother at the time. ‘What would we do when he’s discharged from hospital?’

‘He hasn’t been injured yet. If he is, we’ll cope … we always have.’

Without appearing to listen Susan continues, 'and those that have suffered gas attacks are worse: spluttering, chocking, vomiting – it's awful. And the others with shell shock are worse still, I'm told. They keep them separate you know. I expect their looks and habits would upset the other patients. They're posting me to that wing next week. They keep them away from the public: too upsetting. It's like being in a ward full of 'loonies'. Susan busies herself in the kitchen while continuing her rant. 'It's pitiful. The poor blighters can't help it. Some writhe on the floor, others can't speak and their eyes appear to stare at you in a manic sort of way. Another thing, whenever they hear a noise they go to ground, pulling the bed clothes over their heads or actually crawling under the bed; it's heart breaking, it really is'.

Beryl realises her daughter has to talk about it, get it off her chest before she becomes morose. 'Oh, thanks for that. That's just what I want to hear prior to your dad arriving home and then going off to the Front. Anyway, how do you know this? You haven't seen them yet.'

'One of the sisters gave us a talk on it.'

'Well, you're not there yet. So give it a rest, let's just look forward to seeing your dad.'

'Sorry, mum. I have to talk to someone else outside of the hospital.'

‘I understand dear, but why are they moving you round so often? They’re not sending you to the Front as well!’

‘Don’t know. We are a bit short-staffed in certain departments, but there’s a rumour that one or two of us might be asked to go as VADs to the hospital at Etaples.’

‘Where’s that?’

‘Near Calais, don’t worry mum. I’ll need a lot more training and experience before that happens. Besides, I want to stay here and finish my nurses’ training.’

Beryl Cooper instructs her daughter not to burden her father with this information about the shell-shocked patients. ‘He’s got enough to worry about and I want him to enjoy himself at the weekend when he comes home.’ Susan agrees.

Beryl wonders what effect this hospital experience will have on her 17 year-old daughter. Susan is an impressionable girl who wears her heart on her sleeve. With her blond hair and deep green eyes, slightly turned up nose and full lips she is attractive; when in or out of uniform, she turns heads: a fact that does not go unnoticed by her mother. Beryl could be described as a comfy version of her daughter; in her day she, too, turned heads.

Mother and daughter spend what spare time they have over the next two days sprucing up the two-up, two-down terraced house, not that there is a great deal to do in the living-cum-dining room with adjoining kitchen. Anyone visiting would think they are preparing for a wedding reception or birthday party. Two vases are displayed on the small sideboard and Susan deposits a newly purchased bunch of flowers in each vase; an exceptional extravagance in this household.

CHAPTER THREE

Private Harry Cooper is looking forward to his embarkation leave – not because he is going abroad to fight, but because it's been several months since he has seen his family; in fact, 37-year-old Harry has never been parted from his wife and daughter Susan for so long. 'I know Salisbury Plain isn't that far but it seems like a millions miles from the woman I love,' he said in his last letter. Beryl is touched by what he wrote. The brief notes and expressed feelings serve to bring them closer together; she keeps all his letters. Prior to the war the furthest he had travelled was the fifteen miles to Canterbury to work.

On advice from some of his pals he enlisted in early 1916, just prior to the introduction of conscription so that he could select which outfit to join. 'Enlist now Harry and you'll have a choice of regiment, conscripts aren't given that option,' they told him. He took their advice and became a member of the 12th (Eastern) Division of The Buffs (East Kent Regiment). Basic training took place at Sandling Camp, near Shorncliffe, not too far from home, where some of his pals were still posted; others had already gone overseas to France and Belgium.

Basic training, as expected, contained lots of marching, drilling, physical training, shooting and digging trenches. Now that he has completed this vigorous training he feels he has been acquainted with practically every square yard of Salisbury Plain.

There are some people who, no matter how much training they receive, will never really become effective soldiers. And for some of the callow youths whose previous existence was working behind a desk it was a very difficult transition. Harry, on the other hand, is built for hard manual work. He is of average height for a working-class man at five and a half feet, with broad shoulders and muscular arms: he is immensely strong. As an ex-manual worker he finds the exertions inherent in the physical rigours of military life pose very little problem. 'I'm going to have to keep an eye on you Cooper,' said the platoon commander. 'Why's that, sir?' asks Harry, wondering if he's done something wrong. 'The sergeant-major and I think you have the makings of being a first class soldier. And being older than many of the other raw recruits, and married man to boot, means others look up to you. We noticed that the youngsters go to you first if they have a problem.' Harry Cooper felt quite chuffed about what the platoon commander had to say, although he is wary of undermining the authority of the NCOs and officers. On one occasion he spotted a very young conscript in distress and, because of his age and manner, was able, if not to sort out the youth's problem, to comfort him and explain how the boy's parents must be feeling. The youth responded to Harry's fatherly advice.

The Army, or rather the war, has perversely been a 'blessing' to some people. First it means that Harry Cooper has full employment, something he rarely experienced during the winter months in peace time, and the three incomes mean the family finances have increased substantially. His health has improved now he is physically fitter and medical treatment is free. However, it is not only Harry who has benefitted from the war. It means that now his wife and his daughter have a job, the whole family is experiencing an unprecedented degree of security.

When Beryl asked why he volunteered he replied, 'how can I stay at home when you two are doing war-work?' Harry was also aware of the rumours regarding conscription.

The hiss of steam and clanking of breaks heralds the next stop. Harry Cooper clambers out of the carriage and bids farewell to his pals. He is clad in full marching-order, complete with large and small packs, ammunition pouches, water bottle, tin hat, bayonet and rifle. His kit bag has gone on ahead, with the remainder of the contingent's equipment to Folkestone, ready for loading onto the troop ship in a few days' time.

It isn't too far to walk home, two or three miles are nothing to a fit infantry soldier. The house is the last one in a row of red brick workers' cottages. It is rented. The Coopers hope that with the additional income, they can afford, in the not too distant future, to move to a larger, more comfortable dwelling. The present two-up-two-down tenement is damp and cold in the winter months. Lighting consisted of gas lamps downstairs, paraffin lamps and candles upstairs - electricity has not yet reached this part of the countryside. Cooking is done on a kitchen range. The toilet is at the bottom of a small garden.

Tragedy struck early in this family when Beryl miscarried their first born, a boy who was to be named Earnest. Beryl and Harry were then in their teens and the marriage was a hasty affair as the wedding had to be organised prior to the birth. The thought of producing an illegitimate child was not to be contemplated by any self-respecting family. A year later their daughter Susan arrived. That was eighteen years ago. Harry felt particularly touched and quietly emotional when reading Beryl's last letter. The prospect of a long separation heightened the emotion. In the letter she referred back to their son's death saying 'do come back Harry, I've lost one precious boy – I don't want to lose another': this shared tragedy touched a nerve.

Harry whistles to himself, oblivious to the rain as he marches briskly along the lane and around the corner. He stops for a moment at the top of the hill and looks down the concave slope towards the terraced row of cottages. Smoke emanates from the chimney of the first house. It is a welcoming sight, an indication someone is at home.

Susan comes from around the back of the house, struggling with a full coal scuttle when she notices the soldier walking down the hill. She needs no second glance to distinguish the person's gait. The scuttle is dropped and she runs up the hill to hug her dad.

Beryl hears her daughter's shouts of delight and goes to the door ready to embrace her husband. Standing back she explains, 'My, Harry, don't you look the model soldier! You've lost weight, got a bit of a tan and look really fit.'

'It's all that marching and digging.'

'Oh, I'm glad you said that. The veggie patch out back could do with turning over.'

‘You’ve got to be joking! I’ve got better things to do first,’ says Harry kissing his wife and giving her a passionate squeeze.

‘Now then, what do you want first … what about a cup of tea?’

‘That will be lovely. Then some grub and then a whole bit of loving. I think our lovely girl will have to make herself scarce for a while.’

‘Don’t worry about me you two old love birds … I’ll be off to work later.’

It is nice being fussed over by two adoring ladies thinks Harry. His two blonds, ‘my curvy wenches, my pair of English roses,’ he fondly calls them. The women are comparable in height both standing at about five foot three.

‘This is a sight better than being shouted at by NCOs, and eating out of a mess tin in the open with the wind howling and the threat of rain’, comments Harry.

You don’t eat outdoors all the time, do you?’

‘No dear, there is a Mess hall at the camp but it’s rarely used by troops in training; most of the time is spent on the hills either marching or wielding a pick and shovel, digging trenches, shooting on the ranges or sometimes lobbing dummy grenades'. Home is bliss, albeit temporarily.

The morning comes and Harry takes great delight in having a lie-in, but then he sits up and asks in a concerned tone, 'Don't you have to be at work today Beryl … you won't get into trouble staying at home … will you?'

'You stay there dear and drink yer tea.'

Harry is used to being up at the crack of dawn and is soon washed and dressed.

Reiterating his concern, Harry again inquires 'I hope you won't get into trouble being at home. You can't afford to lose your job.' He emphasises the point before taking his place at the table.

'Don't worry. The boss may be a hard task master when it comes to work, but he always allows us a day off when he knows someone in the family is going to the Front.'

'Well, that's big of him! So what are we going to do? It would be nice if the three of us could go somewhere together. It'll be my treat.'

'In that case let's think of somewhere grand.'

‘What about a night out at the theatre? Let’s go to the Hippodrome.’

‘What’s on? I don’t want to go to another one of those military plays. You know the ones, *The Man Who Stayed at Home* or *The Hem of the Flag*: I hate them.’

‘I agree with mum, they’re full of unbelievable rubbish. The British always win and never get hurt. Oh yes, and if they are maimed in any way they experience a miraculous recovery by the end of the play; I can assure you that rarely happens. Those playwrights want to come to the hospital and see the reality.’

‘I thought you were going to work.’

‘I am, dad. I am. Bye.’

‘Bye love.’

‘Well, I don’t want to see a play about the Army – I’ve seen enough of that these past months’. Beryl looks through the paper. ‘There’s a variety show on at the Hippodrome. We’ll hop on a train to Margate,’ she says.

‘Right, that’s settled then.’

A trip out together with the whole family is a rare treat, especially in war time. The train pulls into Margate station and the Coopers make haste along the sea front and up Marine Terrace to the Georgian splendour of Cecil Square to the Hippodrome Playhouse. There is always an air of expectancy on the way to a theatre, a sort of group engendered excitement.

The programme promotes the usual supporting fare: conjuror, ventriloquist, a balancing act, dancers, comedian and singers. But the highlight for the Coopers is the return on stage of the male impersonator. She is dressed, as is the custom during these days of war, in a military uniform complete with riding boots, tunic, Sam Browne, cap and carrying a swagger stick – in the style of the more famous Vesta Tilley. The audience join in by singing the chorus to: *It's a Long Way to Tipperary*, *Keep the Home Fires Burning* and *Pack up Your Troubles in your Old kit bag*. It is her final song that elicits the greatest response as she sings the song to the 'principal girl', and the remainder of the cast help to swell the vocal effect. It is, of course, *If You Were the Only Girl in the World*.

Beryl grips Harry's arm tightly. He squeezes her hand as if to reassure her; both know what is to come. Will he come back? Dear God, she hopes so. Susan is aware of her parent's feelings and in an effort not to encroach on their private moment looks around the theatre. The response seems to be almost universal, with couples getting closer. Not surprising really as half the audience is in a khaki or blue uniform; a large contingent come from the local Naval Base at Westgate-on-Sea and the Army flying base at Manston. Others, like her dad, are individuals either on their way to the Front or recuperating on sick leave.

Glancing around Susan notices a dark-haired young man looking at her. He is seated in one of the boxes above and to the side of the stalls. He appears to be a similar age to her. She is pleased and flattered to have this attention, but he is not a total stranger. She has seen him before, but where? Beryl notices her daughter's preoccupation with the fresh-faced, youthful looking man. Seeing the puzzled look on Susan's face she says, 'Don't you remember him?'

'He is handsome, mum.'

'You mean he's still handsome.'

'What do you mean? I don't think I know him … but there's something familiar.'

'You remember the time when you came to meet me at the factory, and this lad got out of the boss's car?'

'Oh, yes!'

'You wondered if he saw you. Well, now you know. He did, and you obviously made the right impression.'

James Hemmings now has eyes for Susan. The seeming anonymity of being among an audience gives him the courage to mouth the words of the song:

'*If you were the only girl in the world*
  and I was the only boy
Nothing else would matter in the world today
  We could go on loving in the same old way.'

By this time the two youngsters are, in effect, singing to each other. It is fun and at the end of the song they both dissolve into giggles. The woman sitting next to James – probably his mother thinks Beryl – jerks his arm and appears to get his attention away from Susan.

On the way back to the station Harry and Beryl walk arm in arm, while Susan muses about the boy; 'he's handsome and he's in good working order, unlike most of my patients,' she says. She mentally reprimands herself for thinking such disingenuous thoughts, but hopes to see him again; it is thought to be unlikely. Her mother, although aware of her daughter's possible interest in Mr Hemmings' son, decides that this is not the time to discuss the possible disadvantages of being attracted to her boss's offspring.

The day after next the air is sombre in the Cooper's household. The jollity of the theatre has given way to the reality of Harry's pending departure.

'Have you got everything Harry?' asks Beryl.

'Yeah, I've checked it twice.'

Beryl is feeling redundant. Apart from washing some of his clothes, he would not allow her to iron his uniform, insisting on doing it himself. She feels that she has nothing to contribute; she isn't familiar with army uniforms and kit. Harry tightens his puttees, clips on his belt with scabbard, complete with bayonet, dons cross straps, pouches, water bottle and carrier, large and small pack, and puts his arm through the rifle sling, hoists his kitbag on to his shoulder. He is now, with rifle over his other shoulder, ready to re-join the Army and march-off to war. Susan has left for her early shift having bid her father a tearful farewell. Beryl accompanies him to the station and sees him board the train to Folkestone.

'Don't forget to write and let me know what you're doing,' chokes Beryl.

'Don't worry, I'll write as often as I can. Can't say how much I'll be able to tell you. Look after our Susan. She's a great kid. Seeing her in that nurses' uniform makes you realise that she isn't a kid no more. Tell Dolly I'll look out for our cousin George. Bye love, look after yerself. Take care.'

There's a last clinging embrace before Harry clambers onto the train and finds an open window to wave to the ever-decreasing figure of his wife. He wants to call out to her but finds it difficult to speak; his throat is tight and restricted by the emotion. He has never seen his wife with tears flooding down her cheeks before: the reality of the situation, the separation and possibility of not returning begins to register.

CHAPTER FOUR

The one and a half hour train journey, including stops at other coastal resorts, where more departing husbands and sons wave strained goodbyes, are moving affairs. Fortunately Harry knows several of those making the trip as they are members of the East Kent Regiment. Boyish banter helps to disguise the inner feelings of family separation. The train passes Dover and soon pulls into what has become the major military port of Folkestone.

Harry forms-up with other *Men of Kent.* Kit bags are collected and slung over shoulders as they march in unison along *The Leas* to the precipitous hill of Slope Road which descends to the lower part of the town, and the harbour.

Harry and his company are ushered aboard and directed below deck. There's a bit of a scramble for a placement on one of the three-tiered bunks. Nobody wants the top bunk as a squaddie from Margate points out, 'It's a long way down when yer bursting for a piss.' And many of them would as they had imbibed quite a bit on this their maiden and possibly last voyage. As soon as the hold is full the iron door at the top of the stairway leading to the deck is closed; not an encouraging sign thinks Harry, especially for anyone suffering from claustrophobia.

There is no opportunity for anyone to wave 'goodbye' to acquaintances on the quayside. Most of the accompanying families and friends have followed the troops down the hill to the jetty, and are greatly disappointed at not seeing their men up on the deck – possibly for the last time. Beryl wanted to come as far as Folkestone, Harry persuaded her not too. He didn't want to be seen being emotionally upset in front of other soldiers – he refrained from admitting this to his wife.

The men are allowed to emerge from the lower decks once the ship is clear of the port. The boys lean against the rails and watch an incoming troop ship. It is not an inspiring sight; the upper deck is covered with stretcher cases. How many more are below decks can only be guessed at. The sight sends a shiver down Harry's spine. A young man standing next to him coughs in such a way as to stifles a sob. Harry gives him a comforting pat on the shoulder and feigning bravado says, 'don't worry son the other ships are full of the fit blokes'. The lad appreciates Harry's gesture and tries to force a smile. This wasn't the first, nor would it be the last time Harry Cooper would be comforting soldiers young enough to be his son.

The waves increase in size as the weather changes and the men get below in order to keep dry. This is the first time afloat for many of them and the undulating motion of the bows results in a large number becoming sea sick, it seemed to affect those on the top bunks worst of all. 'Christ, it's revolting down there' comments Harry to another tommy who, like him, is now leaning over the rails, he is back on deck, not because he feels sick but because of the insufferable stench of vomit down below. Fortunately the crossing is fairly short, only a couple of hours.

On arrival in Boulogne the men are divided into companies and march off to a holding camp before being moved to a place of transit. They spend just a couple of days at the large transit encampment; time enough to zero their weapons, do some bayonet charging and get issued with more kit. Normally newly-arrived troops spend longer here but the needs of the Front Line are dictated by the requirements of commanders, and the war.

On the third day a welcomed extra mid-morning snack of bread and cheese and a cup of tea are readily accepted before entraining on a small gauged railway. This means of transport does not last long, and the remaining leg of the journey is reliant on 'shanks' pony'; a twenty-mile hike. They arrive at their billets in the failing light of early evening.

The billets are outhouses and barns. Harry's platoon is housed in a building bereft of most of its roof: the boys' hope it won't rain; 'This place makes Margate look like Monte Carlo' calls out a wag. Sleeping on a ground-sheet laid out on a stone floor is less than comfortable and ensures rest is, at best, intermittent: something they will have to get used to. Morning dawns and prior to breakfast the men are paraded in a muddy water-logged field to be inspected by a Brigadier-General. The Brigadier, astride his charger, makes a short speech in which he emphasises the importance of discipline in the trenches. They are reminded of the efforts of their forebears in the previous encounters at Mons, the Aisne and the Battle of Ypres. The Brigadier, on completion of what he regards as an inspiring introductory talk, taps his heels against the flanks of his horse and rides away; 'Who the bloody 'ell was that?' says Ken from Dover in mock astonishment. 'A reasonable question,' thought Harry. He often wonders why staff officers rarely considered it necessary to tell you who they are. The red-tabbed panjandrums merely introduce themselves by their position.

"Fortified" by the Brigadier's brief speech the troops entrain for the short trip to the training encampment at Etaples. Not the most encouraging initial stop-over as it's the largest hospital base for allied troops in France and the biggest army detention centre. The few days spent there are brutal. Judging by the mentality and methods of the instructors most of them are employed in the military prison. It is a sort of no-man's-land between England and France where those in charge work to their own rules. It is rumoured that the sadistic instructors have never actually seen action at the Front Line - not that Etaples is immune to aerial bombing. The enemy views the four mile long by two mile wide area as an occasional target; perhaps if the hospitals were in a separate town away from the training area and the shooting ranges, the Huns might be more selective in their bombardment. Time is spent in intensive training involving gas warfare, bayonet drills and prolonged sessions charging across the sand dunes, and firing on the shooting ranges – not to mention the route marches. Harry, along with other members in the company is of the opinion that going to the Front Line might be a welcome change!

After a week of back-breaking training the day of departure arrives and Captain East, the company commander, a young twenty-four year old veteran with two major offensives under his belt, approaches and introduces himself along with other company HQ staff to the recently formed collection of battle-virgin soldiers. Harry Cooper, and the remainder of his new platoon, is handed over to their platoon commander, who in turn introduces them to their platoon sergeant. It is a relief to get away from the brutal training cadre at Etaples, and the damp, crowded bell tents.

A broad shouldered man with a walrus moustache and three stripes on his arm calls the platoon to 'Attention' and introduces himself. 'My name is Sergeant Boneaply. No doubt you will shorten that but hopefully – for your sake – not within my hearing.' Judging by the medal ribbons over his left breast pocket, Sergeant Boney, as he was soon to be referred to, has seen previous service in South Africa during the Boer War. He does not boast or mention this prior combat experience, but he does say that 'this present war is bigger and like nothing else I have ever witnessed.' He then dismisses the platoon for a breakfast break which consists of porridge and bread and butter. All the men are issued with a packet of hard tack biscuits, commonly referred to as 'dog biscuits'. Some complain that due to having less than a full set of teeth, they find them hard to eat; the complaint falls on deaf ears. On the advice of Sergeant Boney they stow them in a pocket for use at a later time 'when rations might fail to arrive.'

There is little chatter; everyone is wondering what will happen next. Background noise on this still and misty early morning is broken temporarily by the rustle of leaves in the wind, and the full-throated chirping of the dawn chorus.

The commander and senior NCOs of the East Kent Regiment are strict, but nevertheless seem more civilised than those hitherto encountered. Soon the company is lined up one platoon behind the other, called to attention and ordered to turn left in fours ready to be marched off. Where to? No one knows; except the company commander. This is par for the course. The troops rarely know where they are going, how far it is, or how long they will be marching.

They set off at a regular cross-country marching speed of 120 paces to the minute. The rhythmic sound of marching is a kind of reassurance to Harry and his pals. A hundred and fifty pairs of hob-nailed boots marching in unison engenders a feeling of togetherness and strength especially to these men new to foreign fields, and to the sounds and smell of battle. At ten miles the company commander, Captain Peter East, halts the column and the men rest on the roadside bank and indulge in a smoke break. It is then they first hear the soon to be familiar noises of war. The spasmodic sound of artillery shells exploding and the faint crack of individual rifle fire is discernible.

'How far to go now Sergeant?' enquires a fresh-faced looking Private Thompson.

'I dunno,' replies Sergeant Boneaply. 'I'm told we're marching parallel to the trenches until we get to our turn- off.

Then we move to the Line, join the remainder of the battalion and reinforce those already there.'

The company sets off by platoon at three minute intervals; they are informed that the separate smaller columns present a reduced target for the enemy.

By way of covering the feelings of creeping anticipation and concern by most and excitement on behalf of some, Sergeant Boney asks if someone can start a sing-along. Men take it in turns to begin a different song. After an extended rendering of well-known ditties and airs, someone shouts, 'Come on Harry, your turn.'

'Blimey, we've been through the whole bloody repertoire!'

'No we ain't. Sing, sing or show us your rin…'

'Alright,' interrupts Harry before they demand to hear the rhyming slang indicating a personal part of his anatomy. The only thing that comes to mind is the song he remembers hearing at the Hippodrome. So he gives voice to '*If you were the only girl in the world ...*' To great laughter the remainder join in '*... and I was the only boy...*'

The lads really enjoy the singing. Corporal Mossy, an ex-costermonger from the London's East End who moved to Ramsgate having married a Kent girl, appears mockingly to take exception to the method of accompaniment by the platoon, and in particular a couple of Privates.

‘Hey Sarge … look at them two … they’re ‘olding ‘ands.’

‘Well perhaps he’s the only boy in the world for him. Don’t yer know the words of the song?’ retorts Sergeant Boney.

‘Yeah, but that’s not part of the Army drill manual, is it? I mean, Presenting Arms is one thing, but holding ‘ands! I mean …’

‘The boys seem to be enjoying themselves,’ chips in the platoon commander, Lieutenant Laurence Griffiths.

‘Yes Sir,’ chimes in Sergeant Boneaply, ‘but Mossy seems to think it is prejudicial to army discipline as it’s not part of King’s Regulations.’

‘I’m sure the King won’t mind,’ replies Lieutenant Griffiths.

‘E might not Sir’, retorts Corporal Mossey. ‘But I’m not sure the King would be very ‘appy having a couple of queens in his Army!’

The singing comes to an end when the occasional bullet is heard whistling overhead. Zip! Zip! The unmistakable sound of rounds thudding into trees and buildings reminds the men, as if they need it, of where they are and where they are heading. Occasionally they are passed on the opposite side of the road by small groups of soldiers going in the reverse direction. The passing troops with heavy gait are covered in mud and tramping back to some given rendezvous point: they only have eyes for themselves; they look dejected and exhausted.

'Gawd, they don't look too 'appy' remarks seventeen year-old Thompson. Have they just come from where we're going?' Harry gives him a comforting grin; there's not much else he could do or say: how the hell should he know.

A little further down the road an officer appears from behind a bombed out building and explains to Harry's fair-haired young twenty year old platoon commander, Lieutenant Griffiths, the problems that lie ahead. The road junction soon to be encountered is being 'periodically strafed by machine gun fire' he announces, loud enough for everyone to hear. A quick 'conflab' between the subaltern and the sergeant results in the platoon taking evasive action. When the junction comes into sight the men cross the road at irregular intervals so as to make it more difficult for the enemy. This hiatus slows down the pace of the march but, fortunately, it means the platoon crosses the dangerous obstacle without incident or injury.

A mile or so further on they are met by the previous occupants of a temporary trench and other members of the East Kent Regiment. There is no time for ‘hellos’. The temporary defence has to be reinforced, and for the remainder of the day the men dig in, increasing the depth of the defensive line, creating a fire step and widening a communication trench. The clunk, clunk of pick and spade, stertorous grunts of men heaving great sods of earth with occasional curses are spasmodically interrupted by the crack of rifle fire.

As darkness falls Harry Cooper and his comrades sit on the fire step and wipe the perspiration from their brows. ‘I hate it when you stop, the cold sweat sends shivers down me spine,’ complains Corporal Mossey. The drop in temperature adds to the soldiers’ discomfort. It is at this point there appear a couple of men with two large tureens, one contains a stew, the other tea; ‘Not before bleedin' time,’ chimes Corporal Mossey. The sight of the arrival of victuals is made twice as welcome as one of the porters is no less than Harry’s wife’s cousin, George – Dolly’s husband.

The cousins embrace and exchange a few words. Others complain that their family reunion is holding up their grub which is getting cold.

‘I’ll catch you on the way back, Harry,’ shouts George as he continues on his rounds.

A few minutes later he returns. 'I wondered if we would meet,' says Harry.

'How's Dolly and me boy Charlie, have you seen 'em?'

'Yeah, they're OK. Oh! Before I forget, Dolly gave me this letter to give to you. She reckoned I might get to see you before the mail arrived.'

'She's right, bless her. It can take some time before letters get 'ere, especially when you're on the move. So don't expect a daily postal service. Well, I ain't going to tell you what it's like. You'll get the idea soon enough when you go on patrol. I'm grateful for the letter, a real treat. Good to see you Harry. Well, got to go and feed some more. Cheerio!'

'Cheerio, George.'

Sergeant Boney walks along the trench, stopping now and again to detail a man to act as look-out, while instructing the others to wrap themselves in their groundsheets and telling them that this is where they are 'kipping' for the next night or two. Sergeant Boney tells Harry 'You are on the first stag Cooper, 2100 to 2300 hours, two hours on, four hours off – got that!' Harry nods by way of acknowledgement.

Sergeant Boney now raises the pitch of his voice so that everyone can hear him, '*DO NOT*, I say again, DO NOT, fall asleep when on look-out, unless of course you want to face a court-marshal. Right, Cooper, put a round up the spout just in case. If you see anyone crawling back to this trench, challenge him, if he doesn't reply, shoot the bastard. Got that?'

'Yes, Sergeant,' replies Harry.

Harry's eyes soon become accustomed to the dark. The scalloped indented landscape is highlighted under the light of a full moon and each water-filled pool becomes a mirror. To the observer it is both an eerie yet wondrous sight, like a scene from an abstract painting.

There is little action for the first hour. Harry begins to think of home. He wonders how Beryl is coping. They have been together for twenty years, ever since they were in their teens. A picture forms in his mind of Beryl, her cheeks hot from working over the stove. Her blond hair is tied back and an apron covers her comely figure. But what worries him is the changing colour of her skin, the yellowness brought on by working with TNT might, he thinks, have a detrimental effect on her health. This concern was not voiced by him when he was at home. She is proud, as he is, to be doing her bit for the country in its time of need. He has no doubt that she shares the unmentioned concern. Besides if she didn't work in the factory what else could she do? The only credentials she has pertain to domestic service, and there is less and less of that these days.

There is some action during the second half of his shift. If Harry listens intently he can hear the odd sound of movement, the periodic click-clunk of metal on metal. Is the enemy trying to clip our barbed wire or are we clipping theirs? He wonders. The trenches are only one hundred or so yards apart, and in the stillness of the night noise travels. The Verey Lights sent up by the Germans indicate that everyone is alert and on the lookout. The flares clearly illuminate no-mans' land and the forward line trenches. The sentries then face the dilemma of looking to see if anything untoward is occurring in no-man's land, while at the same time not wanting to be a target for an enemy sniper. Glances at the killing zone of no-mans-land are brief.

Harry is quite pleased when he is relieved of his duties and someone else takes over for the next two hours. Climbing down from the fire-step he meets an orderly waiting with an urn of tea. Sergeant Boneaply, is also there, he is holding an earthenware jug.

'What's in the jug, Sarge?'

'Hold out your mess tin while I slop a bit of it in there. It'll warm you up.'

‘What is it?’

‘Taste it and see. You’ll like it!’

‘Oh yeah, nice bit o’rum; where did you manage to scrounge that?’

‘No questions, no pack-drill!’

‘Thanks, anyway.’

There is nowhere to stretch out and sleep in this newly reconstructed human channel. Bunk holes in the side of the trench have not been fully dug. Soldiers wrap themselves as best they can in their groundsheets and remain seated on the fire step. It promises to be a long and chilly night.

CHAPTER FIVE

‘You’re late Susan, where have you been?’

‘They turned off all the street lamps, we nearly got lost. There must have been an air raid on … I didn’t hear any Zepperlins or airplanes … there again, you don’t always hear the Zepps, do you?’

'Oh yes … I heard there was a bit of an emergency; apparently the church had to turn off the lights and the vicar had to finish his service with the aid of candles. We even had a Special Constable calling here to tell us to put out the lights.'

'So what did you do mum?'

'What do you think? I drew the curtains open and let in a bit of moonlight; sometimes I wonder about you!'

'No need to, I'm alright.'

'Have you seen that young man?'

'Why do you ask?'

'Because you appear to be walking round in a bit of a daze these days … has he tried to make contact?'

Susan looks a little askance and admits that he has. She knows there is no sense in trying to deny events - her mum can read her like a book.

'He knows your shift times so I expect he was around when you clocked off, and guessed that sooner or later I would be there to meet you. You do realise that he is my boss's son and his family live in a different world to us. His dad is in-charge and I doubt if he wants to be this close to his workers.' Beryl continues in an agitate fashion. 'And how can I complain about things, and take the side of Dolly if you two are canoodling; he'll think there's a spy in the camp. And what I've heard of his wife, I don't expect her to come visiting round here. How long has this been going on? '

'Some time … but I love him and he loves me'.

Beryl sighs deeply, her shoulders drop because she knows what it was like to be young and in love; she remembers the response of her parents. She ended up becoming pregnant and felt she had to get married much sooner than expected. True she wanted to marry Harry whatever anyone else said or thought; there was no problem, socially, as they both came from a similar background: working class. These are unusual times, muses Beryl, and wonders if Mr Hemmings junior will eventually be off to the Front. She didn't like to express all her thoughts to Susan, but believes it might be a short lived affair. 'Is he going to be at the factory for the duration?' Beryl asks. A pointed question, guaranteed to irk Susan.

'His name is James … as you well know … and no, he won't,' said Susan tartly. She looks crestfallen and is reluctant to discuss things further. Beryl persists with her inquiries, 'Is James leaving the factory? I doubt if his parents want him to go … what's happening?'

‘James is toying with the idea of following his passion and joining the Royal Flying Corps. Then last week he received a letter with a “white feather”. That made his mind up. He couldn’t stand being called a coward. And, before you ask, no, I don’t know who sent it.’

‘I’m sorry to hear that,’ replies Beryl who feels genuinely aggrieved for both their sakes. ‘Well, now you’re walking out – in a manner of speaking – I’m sure your young man knows the way here. He’s stopped at this gate often enough.’

‘How did you know I was with him? Have you been spying on me?’

‘Firstly, you sometimes referred to ‘we’ so there must have been someone else. And secondly you have shown, by what you say that you have acquired an added interest in aircraft.’

‘You knew who it was then?’

‘Yes, my darlin’, I’ve known for some time.’

‘How come, are you a detective or what?’

‘I told you. The way you behave gives the game away. Added to which you can hardly keep that a secret at work. I might not have seen you but others have. They can see the way you two looked at each other when you come to meet me, even though you both think you can disguise it. I know what it is like to be in love. I was in your position once, you know. This isn't to say I don't love your dad any more, it's just that we've calmed down a bit. You love the boy, don't you?'

'Yes mum, very much.'

'Well, be careful dear … it may not lead to where you hope.'

'What do you mean? He's not in the Army. He's not going to get killed.'

'No, not yet … Not while he's still working at the gunpowder factory. But he has a passion for flying, you said so yourself. …… So, how long will it be before he stops talking about it; how long can he resist the challenge? I know some of the girls at the factory think he should be in uniform and I've heard what they have to say about him not being in the military. And now you tell me he's been presented with a white feather: can't say I'm surprised.'

'He doesn't have to take any notice of it.'

'No he doesn't, but *he does*. You've seen his reaction. Added to which, you're in uniform, albeit part-time, and I bet that makes him feel he ought to be too.'

‘Well, he has talked about enlisting even though he won’t be conscripted.’

‘That’s not what I’ve heard … the rate casualties are piling up; something you must be aware of; newspaper reports suggests it won’t be long before he’s called-up: he’s the right age.’

Beryl continues preparing the tea but senses the unease felt by her daughter. Susan is a little taken aback by the perceptiveness of her mother. She really did believe her assignation to be a well-kept secret.

Now is an opportune moment thinks Beryl, to reiterate the possible problems inherent in her daughter’s romantic liaison.

‘Sit down and have your tea, my dear and let’s have a chat.’

‘Oh! God’ Susan knows that whenever her mother addresses her as ‘my dear’ followed by ‘let’s chat,’ she is in for, at best a ticking off, at worse a lecture.

‘I know what you’re thinking, but before you get up-tight Susan, this is not a telling-off … or a warning. Well, that’s not quite true. But first, let me ask you a question. Do you think you are the main reason for the boy … ’

‘I’ve told you his name is James, James … why don’t you use his name?’ cries Susan, who by this time is beginning to feel extremely touchy. Her terseness is not because she has misbehaved, rather because her mother is usually right in her analysis of her problems and she knows that any remedy proffered will inevitably leave her feeling uncomfortable.

‘I’ve not used his name because we have not been introduced. So, next time he sees you home, I suggest you ask him in so that I can meet him.’

‘Oh … really, do you mean that?’

‘Yes, but …’

‘I knew there’d be a BUT!’

‘You must remember that his dad is my boss. Now that is not a problem to me but it may be to James’ father, or more likely his mother. You may be able to get along with Mr Hemmings but I recall how his mother ensured that James’ attention was jerked back to the stage, and away from you, when we were at the Hippodrome.’

‘You don’t miss much … do you? I thought you were too busy canoodling with dad.’

'James is more than welcome to come here. However, I doubt if his much "more affluent and important" mum will be keen to invite his labouring-class girlfriend into their large, posh detached house.'

'I'm not ashamed about training to be a nurse … what's wrong with being a nurse?'

'Nothing, but I'm a factory worker and your dad's a Private in the Army; the likelihood is that her son, when he eventually enlists – which may be sooner rather than later – will be an officer. And your dad will be expected to salute him. Do you understand where I'm coming from?'

'Yes, I do. But it won't stop us meeting.'

'I know that. Love is a potent force … just be aware that life isn't that simple. Your relationship will affect others. I think you should chat to James about it and see if he invites you to meet his mum and dad. In the meantime he's very welcome to our humble abode.'

As usual mum is right. Susan is uneasy and becomes determined to find out how James really feels about her, and wonders if he will introduce her to his family. In the interim she accepts her mother's advice and invites James into their home. Within a short space of time it becomes usual practice for him to have a cup of tea before he cycles his way onward and homeward on an evening. James promises that at the next opportunity she will be introduced to his parents. He wants her to meet both of them, and so it will have to be organised when he and his father are free from the factory, at present they are working different shifts.

James wonders how much his father knows of the romance. According to Susan and her mum, all the girls at the factory know so why shouldn't his father know? A time needs to be fixed, but in these days of uncertainly any precisely planned events invariably have to be changed, or postponed.

CHAPTER SIX

The factory workers on the early shift are emerging into the sharp, clean air of the early evening. Some visibly gulp in more oxygen welcoming the refreshing release from the stuffy and restricted atmosphere of the bricked confines of the TNT bays.

Beryl stops and turns when she hears the familiar cry of 'You-Hoo'. It is cousin Dolly exiting the factory.

'Beryl, I've been meaning to ask you. Why is it every time you surface from that dangerous pit you work in, there's that young man standing at the window? With the light behind him, I can't quite see who it is, but he seems to be watching you.'

'Oh, it's James.'

'James … James … you don't mean the boss's boy, James Hemmings?'

'Yes, I do.'

'How do you know him? He doesn't fancy older women, does he? After a bit of mothering, is he? Know what I mean!' says Dolly in her usual half mocking, half jocular manner.

'Can't you guess? Everybody else has worked it out. Who sometimes comes to meet me here?'

'Oh, yeah, I remember … your girl Susan. They're not … you know … going out and that … are they?'

'Sometimes Dolly, for all your wise cracks you can occasionally appear a bit bloody slow.'

'Well I never! I'd better be careful about what I say to you before I have to go and see the boss about any complaints from the shop floor.'

Beryl assures her that she doesn't have to; adding that whenever James comes to her house any talk about work and the factory is strictly off the agenda. She reminds her cousin that when they were her daughter's age the only topic that really concerned them was their current boyfriend.

On the mile or so walk to the station Dolly cannot help but interject with 'Well I never, who'd have thought of that!' and other similarly recurring phrases. Finally, by the time they arrive at the station Beryl has managed to change the subject by asking Dolly about her husband George. She is eager to hear news, as she has not heard from Harry for some time.

'Don't know if you've heard? George and Harry met up in the trenches. Yeah, George was delivering the post and Harry gave George the letter I asked him to deliver.'

'Nobody told me … well, how is he?'

'He's OK. As it happens they met up again a couple of weeks later at a regimental concert. It turns out your Harry was a bit of a star.'

'No … Really?'

'Yeah, George said that old Boney – that's Sergeant Boneaply – got up on stage. He had a tutu on and a blue wig. Can you imagine it?'

‘I don’t know this Sergeant Boney.’

‘Yes you do. He was at the variety shows at the Hippodrome in 1915. He was the recruiting sergeant. You couldn’t miss him. He is large and square with a big moustache, looks like the cartoon character from the Old Bill sketches’.

‘Apparently he was a real laugh and when your Harry come on stage, the pair of ‘em bought the ‘ouse down, and then when your Harry sung the song *If you were the only girl in the world* to Sergeant Boney … well, George said they were rolling in the aisles.’ The women laugh.

‘You wait until I see him,’ chuckles Beryl. That’s our song. He’s no right singing it to anyone else, no matter what rank they are.’

The women alight from the train at Westgate and wend their separate ways home, happy in the knowledge that their husbands appear safe at this time, and also happy in the knowledge that they have a kindred family spirit.

Beryl is still feeling highly amused at the thought of her husband singing the song to his sergeant, and can’t wait to convey the news to Susan; after all she and James regard it as their song too.

CHAPTER SEVEN

'Hello mum,' says Susan entering with a pleasing grin on her face.

'Hello dear, you look happy,' replies Beryl. 'Been anywhere nice with James?'

'Just for a walk down to the coast … you know.'

'Yes dear, I do,' Beryl replies in a friendly and knowing manner.

'What's that look supposed to mean?'

'It means I bet you didn't walk too far … judging by the grass on the back of your coat!'

'Mum!'

'It's alright Susan, I'm not being critical. I'm just happy that you're enjoying yourself in these dark times. You never know how long this bloody war will last.' Then added 'but be careful.'

'I don't know what you mean?' replies Susan with a mocked look of innocence. Quickly changing the subject she asks, 'it sounds as if you have heard from dad? Do tell … how is he?'

‘According to our cousin Dolly he’s OK. He’s even been on stage singing a duet with his sergeant.’

‘What did he sing … don’t tell me … it wasn’t *If you were the only girl in the world*, was it?’

‘It was. I think you might be singing it again, only it will be to a young officer. Am I right?’

Susan doesn’t answer straight away. She has that far-away look in her eyes as she recalls her evening with James. They had met by the Guild Hall in Faversham, having decided that it was better to meet away from the factory so as to stop tongues wagging. They wanted a little privacy. It was at the end of the earlier shift and they decided to take a stroll along the lanes towards Boughton Hill. The couple ambled through an orchard and passed the sweet smelling chestnut trees before ascending a steep incline and up through the woods. There they sat and enjoyed the seclusion of the shaded undulating uplands. A view that they each knew they would not be sharing for much longer.

Susan was remembering the conversation she and James had. Clearly James was preoccupied with other things. In an effort to prompt him to talk, Susan broke the silence.

‘You know I love you James’.

‘Yes darling, I know that and you know that I shall always …’

Susan puts a hand to his lips, stopping him from continuing. ‘James I have something to tell you … please listen. You know that I’ll be a fully qualified nurse by the end of the year, and,’ she adds hastily ‘they are looking for volunteers to serve in the hospital at Etaples.’

‘Are they?’ retorts James. ‘Is that meant to be a hint to me?’

‘No, James.’ Susan pauses before taking in a breath and continuing ‘I’m just telling you how it is, and letting you know that I shall be nursing full-time and that I may volunteer to go abroad.’

James has become very sensitive to his position as a non-combatant, albeit with a war-time role. The ‘tut-tuts’ of disapproval from some of the girls at the factory are getting more frequent. No doubt many have boyfriends, brothers or husbands at the Front: he feels that their questioning glances are thus justified. And the proffered white feather lends weight to his misgivings regarding his non-combatant role. But more importantly to him, and unbeknown to them, his desire to don uniform and fly is becoming increasingly more compelling. In a way this prior knowledge of Susan’s possible departure to the war-front confirms his decision to enlist, despite protestations from his father and in particular, from his mother.

‘In case you must know I have had a chat with a couple of the pilots at Manston, and I’ll be calling in to see the station commander soon to get some more information.’

‘Does your mother know?’

‘No, not yet, I’m waiting for the right moment to tell her.’

‘Why is she so against you joining the Army when all your friends have already gone?’

‘Dad reckons it’s because she lost her first child and she doesn’t want to lose another one.’

‘Oh, I didn’t know that; but you’re not a child. When did she lose your sibling?’

‘Two years after the baby was born. My sister died of diphtheria, and according to father my mother never really got over it, hence she appears to be a bit over protective towards me.’

‘I see, that’s explains things. My mum lost a baby too. It was stillborn, not quite the same I know, but still very painful.’

‘Does your mum know about you going to France?’ inquires James.

‘No, not yet, but I’m going to tell her even though it’s about a year away. Anyway, I think she and I need to see dad at home on leave before I make a final decision.’

After a pause she hesitates before continuing ‘James, I don’t like to ask this, but you wanting to go … it’s not really because I might be going, is it?’

Well, let’s just say it helps me make my mind up. You know I’ve had a white feather; you don’t know who it’s from, do you?’

‘No. So what? It’s not that important is it! Anyway, I know you’re keen on flying.’

James is beginning to sound very irritated, ‘Of course it is important; no man wants to be called a coward – does he!’

‘I’m sorry … sorry,’ says Susan giving him a placatory kiss. James shrugs, but finds it difficult to be angry with Susan for long.

Where the couple are sitting gives them a scenic view through a clearing towards Canterbury. ‘Whenever I think of this view I’ll think of us,’ says Susan smiling sweetly. They embrace again. James' affection is becoming more ardent. 'I do love you Susan.'

'Yes I know, but …'

'But, what?'

'I'm frightened James … I don't want to be in the same condition as my mum. I want us to marry because we love each other and not because we have to. And in any case I haven't even met your parents yet.'

The encircling trees shield them from the temperate evening breeze. They lie back down on the green grassy slope. A nightingale circles overhead; despite the increasing emotional desires they are at peace with each other in a turbulent world, at least for the time being.

Back home Susan is roused from her recollections of the day by Beryl's significant cough which indicates that an answer is required from her daughter.

'Oh, yes. Sorry, I was miles away.'

'Still on a grassy bank I expect.'

‘Mum, in answer to your implied question, James will be enlisting but not yet. He’s waiting for the right moment to approach his parents.’

‘You mean his mother?’

‘Yes. Did you know she lost a baby girl, the child was just two years old?’

‘No. But I know how she must feel – that explains a lot, and what about you? What are you going to do when he goes into the Army?’

‘Wait, like everybody else.’

‘Hmmm!’

CHAPTER EIGHT

Morning breaks and the mist rises from the dew-laden, pock-marked countryside of no-mans’ land. ‘Stand-to, stand-to’, shouts Sergeant Boney. Men clamber onto the fire step and peer through the slits in the trench wall. No doubt the enemy is doing the same. Attacks invariably take place when men are at their most vulnerable; either emerging from sleep or at a time when they usually eat: breakfast time is nearly always interrupted. Harry watches a nightingale rise and circle above their heads, and wonders if the same is happening over the fields of Kent.

Action until now as experienced by Harry has been confined to brief but intense periods of shelling during the day. During the hours of darkness time is spent carrying-out patrols, the purposes of which are the cutting of the enemy's wire, patching up and reinforcement of trenches and undertaking reconnaissance. A good night's work is signalled by the capture of an unsuspecting Hun, or two, while mending forward defences. Harry wonders what might happen next.

He doesn't have much time to wait. Shouts are suddenly heard and soldiers are running back and forth along the communication trenches. Harry and his pals stand amazed. 'What the hell's going on?' they cry. Obviously something horrendous is happening. From the oncoming breeze there comes seeping towards the trench, a pungent, nauseous smell; within a few moments the soldiers feel a scratching at the back of the throat and eyes begin to smart. Out of the morning haze now heavy with a greenish tint, comes a patrol. Four returnees stagger over the ramparts and fall into the bottom of the trench.

Corporal Mossey, the patrol leader, tumbles down onto the wooden duckboards, coughing and spluttering. Another soldier is writhing at Harry's feet. They have never seen anything like this. Sergeant Boney arrives, immediately grabs the Corporal and attempts to pour water down his throat, yelling to everyone to get their gas masks on. Lieutenant Griffiths, platoon commander, comes running, sees the situation, beckons to the stretcher bearers behind him to get the affected soldiers away down the nearest communication trench A.S.A.P. Then he signals to the men to follow him away from the line, at the double, to an area out of reach of the poisonous gas.

Numbers are checked. The wind fortunately veers eastwards and apart from Corporal Mossey's party little injury occurs. They all feel compelled to drink copious amounts of water while covering their eyes until they stop smarting. When most have recovered from this first brush with the frothy killer, Captain East, the company commander, calls them together. He instructs the men to form a line and dig themselves in. There they stay, for the remainder of the day, in their hastily constructed temporary defensive position.

Later that night the order comes to withdraw. The company forms-up and marches until dawn breaks, before stopping in the lee of a hedge. They grab what sleep they can. Two hours later they are on the road heading back towards Ypres, finally meeting up with a Scottish regiment. They too had made a hasty retreat from the nascent toxic attack. The respite is welcome as is the much needed food and drink.

Sergeant Boney is shouting commands and Harry with his pals form four ranks on the road. 'Fix bayonets' shouts the Sergeant, 'you never know what or who you might meet around the next corner.' Lieutenant Griffiths checks that every man has his gas mask, commenting, 'we don't want to be caught out again.'

Captain East steps forward and addresses the company. 'We're all tired and weary and want nothing more than to rest. However, there are blokes over there more knackered than us and they need our help. Hopefully we may not have much to do, on the other hand be prepared to do your best: they would do the same for you.' And then, as if to remind his troops who they are and what is expected, he utters the regimental mantra, 'Steady the Buffs'. Whereupon the boys pick up the pace along the dusty road – to where? No one really knows.

In a short while the company swings left down a dirt track that leads to a canal. The approach is along the south side of a steep bank. They can't see what is going on the other side, but the rattle of automatic machine gun fire and the sound of mortar shells exploding give a good indication. After re-sheathing their bayonets they spend the rest of the night ferrying supplies of ammunition, and other equipment to a gap in the bank for collection by the forward troops away on the other side of the fortification.

It is expected that the East Kent unit will relieve the recipients on the further side of the bank, so it is in their own interest to get as much of the supplies up to the Front as possible. The evening temperature drops rapidly and the ground freezes hard: the sweating troops are left aching with cold. The morning, and with it the longed for warmth of the sun, can't come quick enough for Harry and his comrades.

As day breaks the remaining cold rations are devoured and tea is brewed. A welcome sight is the arrival of Corporal Mossey – he has recovered from the gas attack – it was not as serious as first expected. But more important, Harry's cousin George Smith arrives with the mail.

'Hello cus, anything for me?' asks Harry.

'Ere you are Harry, me boy.'

'Ta, I've been looking forward to receiving news. I haven't heard from Beryl or our Susan for bloody weeks.'

Silenced descends along the line as men are engrossed in reading about family and friends. It is the one time when men are, when possible, not interrupted; the letter, the connection with home means so much to the soldiers. A glance to Harry's left reveals the varying responses to the missives. Some smile, others laugh, while a few close their eyes and lean back against the side of a trench and depending on where they are, and the news received, they picture the imagined scenes back home. Harry's eyes are arrested by the sight of tears rolling down Corporal Mossey's cheek. An unlikely response for a man who has seen more action than most and who has proved himself to be an accomplished warrior. Or perhaps he is still suffering from the gas attack? Harry makes his way to the disturbed junior NCO.

'What's up Moz, are you alright? What's the problem, pal?'

'No problem Harry boy.'

'Well, why are you looking upset?'

'I ain't upset, I'm bleeding happy.'

'Really!'

'Yeah, I'm a dad. I got a little toddler … the misses has had our first baby.'

'Great news, congratulations old son'.

'No, it ain't a son, it's a girl. Jesus, I hope I live long enough to get home and see her.'

Harry puts his hand on Mossey's shoulder, the men embrace. Not an action they would normally take, but in the circumstances it seems appropriate seeing that Harry is a father, and therefore understands how Mossey must feel. He leaves the new parent to read his letter over again and again.

Harry returns to his place next to George. 'How's Dolly, alright I hope?'

'Yeah, but I worry about her. Don't you worry about Beryl? Especially since they had that explosion at one of the gunpowder factory sites in Faversham; nearly a hundred killed you know.'

'I know. But that was last year. Beryl says it was a one-off and safety measures have been tightened up. I must tell you, I've got a bit of good news. At least I think its good news. My Susan has a boyfriend. Funny, isn't it? I want her to be happy and settle down but I can't help feeling a bit jealous.'

'Do you know the boy?'

'Sort of, I haven't actually met him but I know of him. He's the son of our Beryl's boss. He works at the gunpowder factory.'

'So why isn't he in the army like the rest of us?'

'Don't really know but according to Beryl, he soon will be.'

‘Is he in training?’

‘Don’t know, think so’

‘Hey, if he becomes an officer, you’ll have to salute him.’

‘Yeah, I hadn’t thought of that. Well, I’ll cross that bridge if and when I come to it.’

The family revelry comes to an end when Captain East orders the platoon gets ready to move, and advance through the gap to the other side of the embankment. The out-going regiment is mighty pleased to be relieved.

The exchange is carried out under cover of the early morning mist, Harry and his cousin George, who is now serving in the same platoon, is reminded of early morning journeys to work across the farmlands of The Isle of Thanet. The mist gathers in patches; one minute the area is clear, next it blankets the fields. The constant alteration of atmosphere engenders feelings, if not of fear then apprehension. Men move in a more crouched position wondering if the mist is heralding danger, or perhaps shrouding their own manoeuvres, hence aiding their protection.

CHAPTER NINE

The dismal blanket of dampness spreads from the continental flatlands across the Channel to the south-east counties of England. It is easier in the winter months to empathise with those at the Front just twenty or so miles across the water, at least in terms of the weather. This miserable atmosphere, exacerbated by the fact that Dolly has not received a letter from George for some time, is reflected in her feelings of disquiet. But that's not the only reason for her unsettlement. She and many of her co-workers have, for some considerable time, been harbouring a grudge regarding what they consider to be unfair working practices: the main bone of contention, as always, is to do with pay. Dolly, the elected shop representative, has that look of determination with a hint of belligerence about her as she heads up the steps to Gordon Hemmings' office. Dolly is built for confrontation. She is squat in physique with a pugnacious face which, when in good humour, breaks out in an atlas of wrinkles and a broad smile, but when aroused she looks dark and brooding, her mouth tightens and furrows appear on her brow. Today is a dark day. She ascends the stairs and is brandishing some papers.

'What's up with her?' enquires Beryl.

'Don't try and stop her this time. She means business,' Says one of the girls.

‘What business?’

‘Our business, she’s trying to get us more money.’

A quick rap at the door to the manager’s office and Dolly Smith – spokesperson-cum-female agitator – strides straight in. ‘What’s the meaning of this?’ demands Mr Woods, the physically overbearing foreman moves across the room and stands defiantly in front of the manager’s desk.

‘I’ll tell you …’ Before she can complete the statement, Mr Hemmings stands up and peering over the foreman’s shoulder asks her to close the door prior to inviting her to sit down. Mr Woods moves to the side of the manager’s desk; his tight strained lips indicating that he is not at all happy. He thinks that she – a worker from the shop floor – should remain standing in the presence of senior management.

‘Now’, continues Mr Hemmings, ‘I want to hear what you have to say, but I want to hear it in an atmosphere of mutual respect, I want us to have a civil and sensible debate.’ This introduction has a calming effect on the diminutive Dolly, now seated; the same cannot be said for the foreman.

‘She hasn’t shown much respect so far, bursting in here without waiting to be told to enter,’ snaps Mr Woods.

‘Mr Woods, please do not interrupt and allow me to conduct the meeting,’ is the stern retort from the boss.

Mr Hemmings is a skilled negotiator. He has been, after all, before he went into the merchant navy, a very successful salesman and is used to dealing with difficult and awkward customers. Dolly is delighted that the overbearing cantankerous foreman has been put in his place and that she appears to be given preference over him.

‘I think you know why I am ‘ere Mr Hemmings. On behalf of the women workers I’m asking for a pay rise. We can’t exist on what we are being paid. You know the cost of living ‘as gawn up since the start of war, and most of us ‘ave families to feed. I have a young son and some of the women ‘ave several children to feed, as well as themselves. I’m afraid we will ‘ave to take industrial action, and believe me, if needs be, we will.’ Dolly Smith, the girl from the East End of London, is nothing, if not blunt.

Mr Woods cannot contain himself any longer, ‘We’re at war! This is not the time to haggle over extra pay. Would you jeopardize the lives of the men at the Front by threatening a go-slow – which, may I remind you, is illegal – just for the sake of a couple of bob. You already get compensation; two bob a week extra for working here.’ And in an effort to vocally ram home his point adds, ‘How are those men in the trenches going to fight without ammunition and armaments?’

Mr Woods' outburst reminds Gordon Hemmings of the thirty-six hours he spent in France. The War Office propaganda and public relations department worked overtime, particularly prior to the introduction of conscription in 1916. Periodically people of note and usefulness were invited to visit the Front. First it was politicians of all parties and men of industry such as steel magnates, then representatives of the Welsh miners, and others such as Gordon, who produce munitions. It was a public way of recognising the importance of their work and the continued need for their support. However, the designation 'Front' was a bit of a misnomer. The munitions delegation did not actually visit a trench or a unit too close to the Line.

Gordon had sailed from England on a late Friday afternoon and disembarked in Boulogne. The delegation was immediately whisked off in a convoy of two staff cars to one of the three chateaux near Field Marshal Haigh's HQ, at St Omer. The location was some sixty miles behind the action. One of the villas was for the Commander-in-Chief and his staff, another for accredited war correspondents and the third for industrial V.I.Ps. An evening meal was provided complete with waiter service. The following morning they were taken to a hospital and shown the effect the enemy's munitions had on our troops. It was a crude effort to emphasise the importance of the need for retaliation with what our munitioneers produce. The afternoon's itinerary included a visit to a munition depot, the size of which was staggering. And lastly they witnessed a demonstration of experimental weapons. A final meal was enjoyed in the safety of the chateau before being driven back to Boulogne.

A couple of the delegates were impressed and delighted to have been given the chance to visit the 'Front'. But most realised that what they saw, although interesting, was several steps removed from the killing grounds. Mr Woods reminded Gordon Hemmings of those delegates, who no doubt would, on arrival home, embellish their reports and claim to have visited the front-line troops. Mr Hemmings nodded in agreement with Mr Woods' comments. Nevertheless, at the time, he did report to his workforce, and used the experience as a means of reminding them of their role and importance.

Dolly stands up and braces herself before addressing the foreman. 'You don't understand do yer? Do yer really think the owner of this factory is concerned about that? The profits amount to millions; he's making more money than ever, and at whose expense? Ours! It's the same everywhere; the miners 'ave been on strike and other munition workers 'ave taken action.' Brandishing the newspapers in her hand she adds, 'And I've got evidence to prove it.'

Mr Woods is now truly incensed. 'Do you want soldiers and sailors to lose their lives for the want of gunpowder and shells?'

‘Need I remind you, Mr Woods’ says Dolly, her voice rising an octave, ‘that the two shillings a week extra we get is danger money, and may I also remind you that last year we buried sixty-nine people here in Faversham as a result of an explosion at the Explosive Loading Company down the road in Uplees.’ Dolly’s voice is now reaching a crescendo. ‘It’s not only the fighting man what is risking his life; ‘ave you forgotten that?’

‘Yes, but they were mainly men; the rescuers’ retorts Mr Woods.

‘Only because it was lunchtime and the building was cleared; ‘ad it been another time of the day it could ‘ave been very different. Don’t you see? You and me, all of us at this factory – are not important: its money what really counts. Only the women count even less than you.’

Realising that this debate is getting over-heated and going nowhere, Mr Hemmings intercedes. ‘Right,’ he says. ‘I’ve heard both sides of the argument. Of course, I’m more aware of what the owner thinks than either of you. I have visited the Front Mr Woods – albeit briefly – so I’m conversant with your side of the debate, now would you please return downstairs and ensure that production has not been lost and that the factory is still working efficiently.’

Mr Woods knows it is futile arguing with the manager, he also realises that the owner will have the final say. After emitting a disapproving grunt he leaves the office. Mr Gordon Hemmings waits for him to descend the open staircase before addressing Mrs Dolly Smith.

'Don't think for one minute I'm not aware of your plight. I've read the newspapers as well you know. But you must realise that I too have a boss to please. And in turn he has to adhere to the rules laid down in the Munitions of War Amendment Act which – correct me if I'm wrong – has suspended trade union practices. This means that munition workers, as Mr Woods made clear, are not allowed to strike.'

'You are quite right Mr Hemmings. I'm not talking of actually striking, but if the women were to work to rule, it would be highly unlikely that this factory will meet the output targets demanded by the Government.'

'This could be construed as a possible means of blackmail.'

'It's the only weapon we 'ave. We don't want this to 'appen. Of course we're pleased to be working, but we must think of our families first.'

'What you may not realise Mrs Smith is that The Defence of the Realm Act puts the owner in a very difficult position: DORA gives the Government the right to take over any factory should they deem it necessary. But the owner and I have been in conference prior to this expected meeting, I'm pleased to report he is prepared to offer you a bonus. The more gunpowder manufactured and shells filled, the more money you will get.'

'That's alright for them that fill the shells, you can count them. What about the others? Another thing, if the 'fillers' get paid for doing even more, they'll rush and could become careless and cut corners: what then? Shells would misfire, the soldiers would suffer, and we might have another explosion … only this time it would be in this factory.'

Gordon Hemmings is astute enough to know that the women have a point, particularly as factories in other parts of the country have given their workers a pay rise, albeit in other industries. An unhappy workforce is a less productive workforce: clearly a compromise is called for. After some haggling Dolly Smith agrees, on behalf of the women, to accept a four shillings and sixpence a week pay rise for all female workers, but concludes by issuing a further demand, that – considering they are working twelve hour shifts – they and the men should have one free meal a day. 'I am asking' she adds, 'for no more than workers get in other munitions factories. What the owner offers is a real improvement, but it still means we earn less than the men, despite the fact that we do the same job!'

‘Believe it or not Mrs Smith, I hear what you are saying and have some understanding of your plight, hence I pre-empted what you might report and approached the owner further, asking him about this very point. He has done his homework and the financial offer is in line with settlements agreed in other factories. And, you will be pleased to know, he has also agreed to the additional free meal for those doing a twelve hour shift. I don’t think we can obtain anymore concessions at this time. Alas, people will argue that it is the *man* who is the main bread winner in the family and that you munition workers are better off than you were before the war.’

‘Yeah, but most of us are dependent upon the pay of soldiers or sailors, and as we don’t see them from one month to the next; this creates a problem, and besides which the chances of them returning ‘ome gets less and less. Who is going to pay for the upkeep of our kids in the meantime? And if they don’t come back, what then?’

‘The owner has offered you a substantial pay rise. You will be taking home nearly thirty shillings a week that’s a rise of nearly twenty per cent. I suggest you accept it for now, and perhaps make another approach next year.’

This seems a good ploy to Dolly Smith. She is pleased that Gordon Hemmings has not shut the door on further negotiation.

Later in the day Dolly speaks to the women employees. As expected some complain that the pay rise is not enough and that it falls short of the men's remuneration, but most praise her for her efforts. Those working long shifts, which are most of them, are grateful for the free meal even though in other factories this was standard practice.

Dolly writes to husband George explaining her achievement. Knowing her character, he is not surprised that she was able to obtain the pay rise and the free meal. He praises her for her success and writes back in jocular fashion, teasingly offering to bring back a sack full of hard tack biscuits for her and her pals to share should the factory meal prove inadequate. He also suggests that she should come to the Front and negotiate with the Generals on the soldiers' behalf!

CHAPTER 10

It's a Friday evening and Susan and her mother are returning from visiting Dolly in town when a special constable shouts for people to take cover from the oncoming Zeppelin, which has discharged part of its dangerous bomb load in the vicinity. A landlord from the hotel on the corner of the road calls to them, 'Come on in, you'll be safer here in my basement'. A second invitation is not needed. They hurry down the steps below ground and enter what is the hotel's social room which is hired out for special functions. It is carpeted and contains an assortment of tables and chairs and a small bar in the far corner. The walls are lined almost exclusively with red-patterned flock wallpaper, and against one end of the room stands an upright piano. Light shines in through two windows looking out to a patio and yard.

By way of introduction the man who had ushered them down the steps says smilingly, 'Let me get you a cup of tea … but before I do … I'm Fred Parting, the landlord. And these good people are …' he gestures, turning to introduce the other seated refuge seekers.

'James!'

'Susan!'

'Oh, you know each other. In that case I'll give my wife a hand with the tea and biscuits,' says Mr Parting, and promptly disappears.

The tall, moustachioed Gordon Hemmings looks every part the middle-class manager; his clothes, bowler hat, stiff white collar and cane match his bearing. He rises out of his seat and stands as if ready to address a group of his workers. He nods in acquaintance to Beryl Cooper saying, 'Well, it seems we can't keep away from one another Mrs Cooper. Moira dear, this is Mrs Cooper. She works for me at Faversham. This is my wife, Moira.' Beryl smiles in acknowledgement.

Moira remains seated. She allows her mouth to turn up at the corners so that her lips form a sort of crease before her look returns to one depicting restrained annoyance. She had heard rumours of James having a girlfriend and was intending to confront him about what might be going on. She intensely dislikes surprises and feels she has been caught out. Judging by the happy response of her son and the delight of the girl, she rightly assumes that they are more than just casual friends.

'We were just catching the sea air and intended to drive to the coast and go for a short walk along the coastal path. We thought some exercise would do us good,' offers Gordon Hemmings by way of an explanation for his family being there.

It appears more of a statement than an explanation; Gordon Hemmings stands as if expecting a corresponding explanation. 'That was partly our intention after visiting my cousin-in-law who you know,' Beryl pauses and seeing the quizzed look on Mr Hemming's face; 'I mean Mrs Dolly Smith, who I believe you met earlier today.'

'Oh, I didn't realise you were related' said Gordon. 'We had a long and fruitful chat. I trust she has conveyed the outcome of our meeting to you and your fellow workers?'

'Yes, she did.'

‘Well, I hope you are pleased with the result of her efforts?’ he says, smiling.

‘Gordon,’ interjects his wife, ‘I didn’t come in here to be embroiled in a factory meeting. Don’t you have enough to do with that during the day? God knows, that’s all I hear about.’

‘You must excuse me, Mrs Cooper. I didn’t want to talk shop but as it is common ground it seems an obvious thing to do. Unfortunately, however, my wife does not share the same concerns we have for the world of munitions.’

‘What about the young lady, are we going to be introduced?’ snaps Moira Hemmings.

Before James can reply, Beryl Cooper, wishing to take the initiative away from Moira Hemmings by seizing the opportunity to introduce the other member of her family speaks ‘This is my daughter Susan. She is presently working at a military hospital in Canterbury – she’s training to be a nurse.’

Susan shakes hands with Gordon Hemmings. A frozen look from Moira Hemmings who turns her head away, suggests that it would not be a good idea to offer her hand to the man’s wife.

‘I assume,’ announces Moira Hemmings, in the manner of a disapproving headmistress, ‘that you have already been introduced to my son.’

‘We have had that pleasure. He has visited our house,’ replies Beryl.

‘Oh! Has he?’ Moira Hemmings retorts waving in an obviously dismissive way, ‘and how come she has not been to visit us?’

At last James feels that this is his chance to have his say, explain his position and assert himself – he doesn’t want to appear ‘wimpish’ in the eyes of his girlfriend. It may also be a means of appeasing his mother.

‘I think you mean Susan, mother. The problem is we rarely, due to dad and I now working different shifts, get the opportunity to meet as a family. I wanted to tell you when we were are all together. That was the reason why I suggested we come out for a drive and a walk this evening. But, as you see, events have overtaken me.’

‘Well, even the best laid plan can go awry my boy,’ comments Gordon Hemmings. ‘You made the effort and your mother and I are grateful for that. Might I suggest that the young nurse comes to tea one day so we might become better acquainted?’ This is an effort on the part of Gordon to raise the status of Susan in the eyes of his wife. 'What do you say, Moira?'

Moira feels decidedly unhappy being caught out, but she has no wish to appear uncivil and so it is a suggestion that she really cannot refuse. She acquiesces, but as is her want, she attempts to have the last word saying, 'I think the comfort of our drawing room would be a much better place to become acquainted than this below stairs basement.'

'This below ground floor room may have saved your life madam,' interjects Mr Parting on entry with the refreshments. Mrs Parting, following her husband, nods vigorously in agreement.

'We'll sort out a convenient date and time with you Miss Cooper – if Mrs Cooper is in agreement.' Beryl Cooper beams while agreeing to the proposition.

'Mr Parting, I hope you do not think that we are ungrateful to you and your wife for providing us with shelter at this time. We really are most relieved to be safe,' concludes Gordon Hemmings. As he did earlier in the day when negotiating at the factory, he shows his mettle in a difficult situation; where others try and bluster their way through, Gordon relies on charm. It usually works.

Mrs Parting, a roundish and jocular landlady is aware of the tension in the room and wishing to help everyone relax, sits at the piano and begins to play softly some of the popular tunes of the day. Looking around at the anxious audience she enquires with a smile, 'Before we hear the All Clear, are there any requests?'

James coughs and asks, 'Do you know the George Robey and Violet Loraine song …?'

'Oh yes; the one from the show, *The Bing Boys Are Here.* How appropriate!' chortles Mrs Parting gleefully. Being a retired music hall artiste she is happy to oblige and begins to sing, *If You Were the Only Girl in the World.* Beryl beams her approval and Susan touches James' sleeve, Gordon smiles, while Moira pretends not to notice.

Mrs Parting completes the song with a flourish and is about to start on another when her husband announces that the 'All Clear' has been sounded. Moira Hemmings immediately stands up. She is a slim woman with angular features and piercing grey eyes. Adjusting her wide-brimmed hat and squarely facing the Coopers she announces to everyone that it is time her family departed. Mr Hemmings again thanks the Partings for their care and protection, James surreptitiously squeezes Susan's hand while ensuring Moira Hemmings doesn't see, and waves a goodbye to Beryl Cooper before hastening after his mother.

Beryl Cooper remains seated and accepts the offered second cup of tea. Mr Parting could not help but mention that he had noticed a certain atmosphere. 'Was it that obvious?' says Susan. 'Yes, it was,' comments Beryl, 'but thanks for the musical interlude Mrs Parting. It helped melt the ice a bit.'

Mr Parting, addressing Beryl, suggests that 'Next-time you are passing, come in and have a drink, and let us know how the young couple are doing – my wife would love to be kept informed.'

On the way home Beryl wonders aloud, how long it will take before Susan is invited to take tea at the Hemmings' abode. Susan assures her mother that she is in no hurry to meet Mrs Moira Hemmings again. 'That may be so, dear. But, if you are as serious about James – as I believe you are – I'm afraid it'll be inevitable. I doubt if you will have any problem with Mr Gordon Hemmings, I think he quite likes you.'

'I wonder what dad will make of James?' asks Susan.

'I'm sure he will like him, but if James is soon to go away with the army the chances of them meeting may be slight. And if they do meet, let's hope it is not in uniform – for both their sakes – as there's quite a difference between officers and other ranks.

What interests me is; how will dad get on with Moira Hemmings?'

'Don't jump the gun, you haven't been invited to their house yet, things might change completely when James is commissioned into the military'.

'Mum, you talk as if he is already in the Army.'

I suspect that he planned to get his parents together for two reasons: first, to tell them about you, and secondly to inform them about his decision to enlist. I may be wrong, but I doubt it.'

'Well, he hasn't yet told me he's enlisting!'

'No, but he's hinted at it, perhaps he thinks it best to get the view of his mum and dad first.'

Beryl and Susan arrive home in good spirits. They feel pleased that they have, at last, met James' family; it was never going to be an easy introduction. At least this way they didn't have to put on 'airs and graces': the truth was there for all to see. Thankfully, they didn't have to socially pretend to be something they are not.

The same calm and placid atmosphere is not discernible in the Hemming's motorcar.   Gordon expresses his delight that

James has found himself a likeable and sensible girl. Moira merely sniffs at this suggestion. James, rather like the Coopers, is pleased that everything is now out in the open and he doesn't have to broach this awkward subject himself. In an aside Gordon tells his son that his mother 'will come round in time'. The fact that Susan is intelligent and is training to be a nurse is a definite plus. However, James has not informed them of his other secret bit of news.

Gordon, as is his way, guesses what is troubling his son. He suspects that, leaving aside the accidental encounter, there is more to this arranged evening out with his son than that which came to light in the basement of the hotel. As they enter their driveway he asks James to come and have a chat in the study before they have supper.

'What secret plans are you hatching now?' inquires Moira. Following the afternoon's revelations, she is feeling decidedly vulnerable.

'It's OK dear, I just want to check up on a bit of business before tomorrow,' Gordon assures his wife.

'Just make sure you're not late for supper,' says Moira.

Gordon and James enter the study. 'Take a seat son. Do you want a drink?'

‘A drink!’ exclaims James, who is a little taken aback to be offered a drink this early in the evening.

‘Well, don’t look so surprised, I know you go into pubs. Anyway, you’re a man now and I believe what you have to tell us about refers to a mature decision that you have recently made. Am I right?

‘Yes dad.’

‘And your decision is?’

James shifts awkwardly in his chair, coughs, looks towards the window and pauses before answering. He is finding the moment very difficult. His father sits keeping his eyes fixed on his son but does not offer to supply the answer, although he is fairly sure he knows what he is about to hear.

‘I’ve enlisted dad.’

Without any emotion Gordon asks, ‘So when are you going?’

‘I’ve been attested, that means I’ve been accepted and I’m now waiting to hear from the War Office. You don’t seem surprised.’

‘I know what being attested means, and no I’m not surprised. I knew it would be just a matter of time.’

‘How did you know?’

‘You’ve always been interested in aircraft and flying, and some of the girls at the factory have been dropping a few hints about you joining the army, even I noticed that. Your school friends have joined up and now your girlfriend is in uniform. I’m aware of the pressures. If it’s any consolation, I’d have taken exactly the same course of action.’

‘You don’t miss much, do you dad?’

‘I don’t need to be a qualified psychologist to work that out, just a concerned father. Of course, I’d rather you don’t go but fully understand why you’ve decided to. The real problem is: how do we let your mother know? She’s feeling as if her nose has been put out of joint at the moment. There have been additional suggestions in the papers that more men are needed, and as you and I know, even if you are in a restricted occupation the chances of an 18-year-old escaping conscription are getting less and less. But there’s now another hurdle to get over.’

‘Yes, I know.’

‘If I were you I’d let your mother get used to you having a girlfriend first, and when the call-up date is known, then approach her about the army. In the meantime let’s invite Susan to tea – at the soonest opportunity.’

‘Thanks dad.’

‘Does Susan know that you have enlisted?’

‘No. I thought it best to tell you and mum first.’

‘It seems quite serious between you two, so I’d tell Susan soonest. I’m pleased you’ve made this choice, to enlist that is. I’m proud of you.’

‘Will you go into the Royal Flying Corps?’

‘I don’t know dad, I have to pass a selection process to see if I’m fit to fly.’

‘I’m sure you are James.’ They raise their glasses.

For the second time today fate has taken a hand and James feels all the better for it.

CHAPTER ELEVEN

The wait for news from the Front is becoming unbearably prolonged, but after several weeks the postman delivers a letter from Harry. Of course he can’t say much, the necessity for censorship sees to that. He has discovered Belgium, he says, in the same way he unearthed Salisbury Plain, ‘with the aid of a shovel'. The main difference is the fields of Belgium are flatter, the chalky hills of the English Southern uplands allows for the rain to drain away; not so in his patch of the battlefield across the channel. In Flanders the fields are a quagmire after prolonged rain: this, complains Harry, makes the job of digging 'a ruddy sight harder.' The only good news is that he has been promoted 'to the exalted rank' of Lance-Corporal. This means he will have a few more bob in his pocket, which he says, 'will be spent on you and Susan when I come home.' Beryl sheds a little tear, which she always does when reading her husband's letters.

She can't help but notice that Harry has changed since being in the army. Of course he's fitter, but that's to be expected. Beryl wonders how he is coping. He's usually a quiet and introverted man but that doesn't mean he can't or won't assert himself when required.

'You remember that time when you 'ad an argument with that toffy-nosed lady when you was working as a maid in that big mansion near Deal', recalls cousin Dolly.

'On yeah, our Harry had a go at her husband and let him know what he thought of the way his lady was treating his future wife.' The problem disappeared almost immediately, alas so did Beryl from that employ – Harry saw to that. 'I was very proud of Harry that day. Mind you I'd 'ave had to leave sooner or later – I was pregnant, not that they knew.'

She now wonders how he is coping with army discipline which is acknowledged to be harsh. ‘Dolly, you know he’s a slow burner, but go beyond a certain point he can quickly lose his temper.’ Then again, Harry needed to be adaptable as he often moved jobs, usually in search of work but also, on the odd occasion, because he gave vent to his temper; ‘he can’t expect to do that in the army’ explains Beryl.

In the summer he worked as a builder’s mate, in the winter he was an odd-job man. He could turn his hand to almost anything to do with wood or bricks; he was known to be reliable and capable, and got on with most people. Beryl thought he should have a full-time job that makes proper use of his capabilities, and one that provides the opportunity of being in charge of others. Perhaps the Army might realise this mused Beryl, and that’s why they promoted him; this pleased her but she didn’t want him to be a soldier for ever.

On reading his letter she, as always, immediately pens a reply. She writes about cousin Dolly’s efforts and the resulting pay rise, and assured him that he has no need to be concerned about spending money on her, as she also got a pay rise. But she does say that she and Susan would enjoy another family night out at the theatre. Central to her news is an account of the happenings in the basement of the hotel during the air raid. She concludes that she thinks he will like James. ‘However, if the boy goes in the Army he’ll be an officer … how do you feel about that? His dad – is me boss –

he's approachable, but I'm not so sure about his mother. She could be a trifle difficult. Anyway, the important thing is, you say you might be coming home. We can't wait to see you again. Susan sends her love. Take care, Love you, Beryl.'

CHAPTER TWELVE

Judging by the column inches in the paper, endeavours on behalf of the military to encourage more enlistments intensifies; recruiting parties are attending theatres, civic functions and sports grounds. It is announced that the upper recruitment age has been raised to forty-one, the height restriction lowered. James is now spending more and more of his free time cycling to the aerodrome at Manston. And Moira is becoming reluctantly resigned to the fact that her only child might soon join the Army; although she is convinced that he is being unduly influenced by this uniformed girlfriend of his.

'You can withdraw, you know – I won't allow your father to give his consent.' She couldn't, of course, carry out this threat; her son is now over eighteen. Besides her husband understands his son's plight and is fully aware of the pressure he is under. Once his enlistment papers arrive, he shows them to his mother: there is no going back, he can't; he is now subject to military law.

James, through premature keenness, is cramming basic necessities into his valise ready for his departure to the training depot in Canterbury when he is stopped abruptly by his mother. 'What are you doing … here let me do that,' she says in an authoritative tone. It was no use James arguing. He realises that it is said out of feelings of concern for him – although she would not admit to the latter. She empties the bag and replaces each item neatly and fastidiously so that the valise now appears only half-full.

'There's no need to fuss mother. I'm not going for another week, and it's not certain that I will be going to Canterbury.'

'I know darling. Believe it or not, I do listen to what you say but you must be prepared. We don't want you turning up late and being on a charge – or whatever it is they call it – straight away.'

'Yes, mother,' replies James in a resigned fashion.

'And while I remember, you will arrange for Susan Cooper to come to dinner one evening before you depart.'

'As if I'd forget, of course I'll ask her to dinner. I'll make doubly sure and give her mother a note to give to Susan.'

'Right, that's settled. Your bags are packed; we are almost ready for you to go.'

‘Are, we? Oh, thanks!’

When referring to James’ girlfriend Moira still insists on using her surname indicating that Susan has, as yet, only got one foot on Moira’s doorstep.

When Susan eventually enters the portals of the Hemmings’ Georgian house for the first time and has been vetted by Moira Hemmings, James, aside to his mother asks what she thinks of Susan. ‘She appears well scrubbed, polite and affable’ was her reply. Moira had invited a couple of ‘socially discerning’ friends for this inaugural dinner in an effort to put Susan under increased social pressure. This rather patronising and crude method of social examination irritates Gordon, but amuses James. Susan had been forewarned that this might happen.

After dinner James, Gordon and the female guests, a deputy head mistress and a governess, depart to the lounge for coffee. Once there Moira’s friends ask Susan all sorts of questions regarding work in the hospital and her duties. She answers with enthusiasm: this pleases the guests. This was not quite the outcome Moira was hoping for. After the ladies and the younger members have left, Gordon suggests to Moira that Susan’s mother, and father – if he is in England – visit their home. ‘Not yet’, said Moira with a finality of tone that defies reply. ‘I understand the girl will become a qualified junior nurse soon, which I suppose gives her junior officer status, and no doubt she has dined out in the officer's mess on more than one occasion.'

'I suppose that means she is partially acceptable where her parents are not!' interjects Gordon. 'I sometimes wonder why you agreed to marry me, Moira. Was it because I had no parents?'

'I'm not in the mood for an argument' retorts Moira, screwing up her face as if in agony; she hurriedly leaves the room.

Unbeknown to the Cooper family the Hemmings had felt compelled to get married in a hurry: becoming pregnant before being wed was regarded as socially disgraceful, particularly among the Victorian and Edwardian middle classes. Moira did not want her son to face the same predicament.

Over the ensuing months Gordon and Moira meet Susan on a number of occasions and they begin to wonder if the romance will progress to the next stage. It is not that Moira dislikes Susan, in fact she finds her quite entertaining, and on one occasion commented that she 'appears to be quite an intelligent girl.' The engrained difficulty, as far as Moira is concerned, is the insurmountable social chasm of her family. Gordon has no problem with this. He recognises his roots.

Gordon Hemmings cannot fail to discern the excitement felt by James pending the young man joining the military. It is reminiscent of the way he used to feel when he took on a new job, a new challenge, and it reminded him of his sense of achievement when he became a junior officer in the Merchant Navy. However, he knows, judging by the list of casualties in the papers, that the odds of his son serving for the duration, and returning home in one piece, may be short.

CHAPTER THIRTEEN

Four months later James and his parents sit around the table in the large dining room waiting for the maid to clear the table. Once done James decides that this is the appropriate moment to announce his intention to ask Susan for her hand in marriage. The response is not one of demonstrative excitement. That is not the way his parents behave. They smile and Gordon offers his congratulations.

'You don't seem at all surprised' comments James. He expects his mother to be more critical.

Moira waits a moment before replying, 'Under normal circumstances this would be considered rather too quick not to say hasty, but these are unusual times. We thought you would ask the question, it was just a question of whether or not Susan Cooper will accept, and when might we hear her reply?'

'When I've had a chance to ask her; we're finding it difficult to find the right moment because of the shifts we both work. I hope she won't refuse.'

'I don't think there will be much chance of that. Anyway, we are pleased to hear it, aren't we Moira?' says Gordon, looking quizzically at his wife. Moira, not wishing to upset her son prior to his departure to the Army, forces a half smile.

'James, you need to talk to Susan's parents and ask her father for permission, although as I understand it you've not met him yet' concludes his mother.

'Well, should she agree you have our blessing but decorum dictates that you need to obtain the permission of the would-be bride's father. Your mother is a stickler for protocol, even in times of war'.

When Moira is alone with Gordon she reiterates her concern about this duel attachment. 'The army should take precedence not his would-be fiancée; are we now supposed to worry about her also?' Gordon attempts to pacify his wife, whilst at the same time empathising with their son.

The following day while walking to the station James halts, looks Susan squarely in the eye and with his usual youthful enthusiasm, excitedly says, 'Susan, I've got a couple of important things I want to say.' Susan is aware of one of the pending announcements; she guesses that James has enlisted. He doesn't need to tell her as his boyish keenness gives the game away. She remembers feeling the same when she began her nurses training; although the 'glamour' of donning the uniform for the first time has begun to fade as she has witnessed some of the devastating effects of war.

This evening, though, he appears more excited and a trifle nervous. In a manner befitting a romantic drama, he drops to one knee and, in an old fashion way, asks for her hand in marriage. She flings her arms around him and readily accepts his proposal and kisses him excitedly. She teasingly giggles and reproaches him for reading too many romantic novels.

With some concern she stutters, 'But … but, have you told your parents? I can't believe your mother is that enthusiastic?'

'Dad says she will come round to accepting my would-be-bride, eventually. At present she is more concerned about me going into the Army. What do you think your parents will say?'

‘My mother’s all for it and I’m sure my dad will agree. He should be home on leave soon, hopefully before you are posted away for training. And don’t forget our parents need to meet first. When I see both of my parents together – eventually – I’ll ensure that they get to meet you, you can be certain of that.’

Susan is overjoyed at being referred to as the ‘would-be bride’, it makes her blush.

A lot has occurred since that day in the basement of the hotel, sheltering from the possible bombing from a Zeppelin. The fact that neither set of parents has visited the other’s home is, in part, a relief to Beryl Cooper. Beryl, in response to her daughter’s doubts, asserts that she can cope with visiting the Hemmings’ large detached house – should she be invited. However, she doesn’t relish the possibility of a reciprocal arrangement; it would only serve to underline their lower status and make her feel extremely uncomfortable. To be honest, it is a state of affairs that both parties understand, and thus neither family want to embarrass the other. For Moira Hemmings it is very important that Susan’s presence has a committed effect on their son, and equally imperative that Susan is deemed intelligent and well-mannered. The fact that Moira’s future daughter-in-law is a qualified professional lady – a nurse no less – indicates that she has ambition and is deemed socially acceptable.

One evening when Susan is at the Hemmings' home and following the announcement of the engagement to both sets of parents, Moira takes Susan aside. They exit the dining room, leaving the men to smoke and chat. 'You know, Susan, he doesn't have to go in the Army, he is after all doing an important job in a reserve occupation.'

'I know.'

'You don't want him to go and fight … risk losing his life … do you?'

'Put like that, no.'

'Neither do I … only one hears about the condition the men are in when they return and I, through my charity work, talk to their relations. But you see the effects of war every day. We don't want him to end up like some of those poor wretches, do we? '

Susan wonders how much of Moira's charity work concerns soldiers. She was sure it wasn't the Women's Emergency Corps as they were the first charity organisation to cater for the Belgian refugees. And she had heard that Moira had rebuffed her husband's suggestion regarding catering for a couple of refugees. It was therefore assumed that it is more likely to be the National Food Fund. Nevertheless Moira no doubt believes that she is doing her bit for the war effort, and this would appease her conscience, so Susan believes.

She is not totally surprised at Moira's not so subtle effort to steer her son away from the military, but she isn't about to ruin the relationship by arguing with her future mother-in-law. Does she, muses Susan, really think by accepting her into the family fold she will have a better chance of persuading James to change his mind? What does she expect her to do? She couldn't possibly tell James not to go when her own father and uncle are out there fighting. Besides which, she doesn't like Moira's inflection, her stress, on the word *wretches* when she refers to the injured soldiers; it sounds as if they are inferior and somehow weak, it sounds cruel, condescending and patronising. But, on this occasion, diplomacy seems the right course of action thus she bites her lip, and refrains from starting a confrontation.

Susan evades Moira's additional employed cunningness to get her way by trying to shift the onus onto her shoulders regarding James' decision to enlist; a method she has employed on more than one occasion.

'I don't think he will listen to me anymore. He ignores his parents' advice. I'd hate him to make a decision that he will later regret. If he does, he'd be blaming you and me for the rest of his life … If he's still got a life,' mumbles Moira.

Although disturbed by what Moira Hemmings is saying, Susan isn't going to let it ruin her feelings of joy. If she's learnt anything by working in the hospital, it is – as all the patients keep reminding her – "live for the moment".

Later in the week as they stroll through Westgate-on-Sea the young couple stop briefly and knock on the door of Mr and Mrs Parting's hotel. It is late in the afternoon and they wonder if they will get a response. They don't have to wait long before the door is opened by the jolly Mrs Parting. She immediately recognises them and calls to her husband. 'Darling come quickly, it's the young ones from the day of the air raid.'

'Come in, come in,' cries Mr Parting.

Shaking his hand James replies 'We won't Sir, if you don't mind, we have very little time but we thought you would like to know the outcome of the brief encounter that occurred here.'

'We are going to be engaged,' chimes in Susan.

‘Going to be, my dears’ chimes Mrs Parting. ‘You either are or you are not betrothed.’ Mrs Parting has a quaint way of expressing herself. She sounds to Susan like someone out of a Dickens’ novel; in fact her comfy figure and ballooning skirt and bib suggested a character from Pickwick Papers.

‘What Susan means to say is that it only remains for me to obtain my father’s permission. We’ll get this when he comes home on leave, shortly.’

‘We are very happy for you both, and should you wish to throw a little party we’d be glad to accommodate you. We’re delighted to have been informed. My wife has been dying to know what resulted from that odd meeting.’ Mrs Parting laughs and spontaneously holds out her arms to embrace Susan. ‘The very best of luck my dears,’ she coos.

The couple thank them for the offer before continuing their amble along the esplanade. The sea is calm and the wintery weather subdued, as is their mood. They are more than pleased that James’ parents are in agreement with their forthcoming engagement. Their acceptance of James’ second bit of news regarding the military is more problematical as far as his mother is concerned: but it is a ‘*fait accompli*’, and so there was no use his mother voicing a prolonged disagreement.

James breaks the silence. 'I had my medical examination at the depot in Canterbury last week and you'll be pleased to know I was accepted. The medical officer said they had to turn many recruits away for being physically unfit.'

'There's absolutely no chance of you being rejected … alas! You come from a healthy, well-fed family, not like some people.'

'Would you mind if I wasn't fit?'

'Yes and no. I prefer to have a good-looking physical specimen for a future husband. On the other hand, if you didn't pass the medical you'd have to stay at home near me.'

'A very diplomatic answer, I must say. By the way I had my first posting orders today. I'll not be joining the East Kent Regiment. I'm to report to the Artists' Rifles HQ in London.'

'But you're not an artist.'

'It's a training battalion. It's where I'll learn the basics: how to fire a rifle, march in step, and dig trenches (in Epping Forest, I'm told) and go on route marches around Thetford in Norfolk. That will last about ten weeks then hopefully it will be off to the Royal Flying Corps.'

'How do you know you will get accepted for the RFC?'

‘I asked for and got an interview with the commanding officer of the flying station at Manston, and he promised to write a letter of recommendation for me.’

‘You’ve got it all worked out, haven’t you!’

‘I did my homework, just as you did before you applied to train to be a nurse. See, you’re already having an influence on me’ he says with a chuckle. ‘I can’t wait to meet your dad and ask for your hand, both for mine and my mother’s sake. My *mama*’ James says with a pronounced posh upper-class accent ‘refuses to announce the pending engagement until social protocol is complete.’ Reverting back to his usual tone, he asks ‘Have you heard from your dad lately?’

Susan mentally recalls the conversation she had with James’ mother about trying to keep him from enlisting. However, she thinks it best not to mention it at this juncture.

‘Dad says there is a lot going on at the moment, but his regiment is due some leave shortly. Don’t worry, as soon as I know the date of his leave I’ll let you know straight away.’

They come to the end of the esplanade and are stopped from going any further by rolls of barbed wire. Their silence is interrupted by the noise of a bi-plane overhead. ‘Ah, a Sopwith Pup powered by a Le Rhone rotary engine with twin 7.7 mm machine guns and a flying ceiling of 17,000 feet …’

‘If I didn’t know you better, I’d say you were a bit of a flying nut … how do you know all that detail?’ jibes Susan.

‘I read about it in a book and they let me look around and ask questions when I visited the air base at Manston.’

There was clearly no debate as to where James’ interest lay, and that in the not too distant future he’ll be up there in the sky. Susan wonders and hopes that he will be stationed nearby at Manston or the nearby Royal Naval Air Service station.

CHAPTER FOURTEEN

A few weeks pass and the couple have settled into a kind of routine. James is spending more of his spare time at the Cooper’s abode – a fact not gone unnoticed by his mother.

Beryl Cooper is eventually invited over for tea one Sunday afternoon. The opportunity to get out of her working clothes and don her best attire is welcomed, but she feels a little apprehensive. The last meeting with Moira Hemmings was not a particularly pleasant experience. She thinks the woman is a domineering social snob. But when she learnt that she had also lost a child Beryl felt a degree of empathy, and now that her own daughter has become an accepted visitor to their house she begins to warm to Moira Hemmings. Her relationship with James' father has always been amicable, even though he is her boss.

James drives his father's car to Beryl's house and takes her and Susan back to the Hemmings' abode. The maid opens the front door and ushers them into the hallway, which in itself is as large as the whole downstairs of Beryl's home. On the left stands a grandfather clock and on the opposite side is the hall table complete with telephone. On the far side to the door is an impressive oak wood staircase. They are directed through the dining room, on the wall of which are portraits of Moira's family, before being led into a conservatory complete with its wicker chairs and matching table; the table is set for afternoon tea. In two opposing corners stand ceramic jardinières with yucca plants, other terracotta pots containing lemon butter ferns are placed next to the French doors, which provide access to the garden. Beryl, although trying not to appear overawed, is nonetheless impressed with such opulence.

The afternoon tea party is pleasant. Gordon is his usual charming self and makes Beryl feel at home. Moira comes across as being a 'mite' possessive when she insists on referring to Susan as 'my future daughter-in-law', the stress being on the word 'my'. But other than that conversation is polite and questions are unobtrusive. Some would say that Susan has done very well for herself, socially.

Later, following the meeting of future in-laws, one of Moira's friends has the temerity to hint to Moira that her future daughter-in-law might be a bit of a 'gold digger'. She is soon put in her place. Moira indicates to the lady concerned that Susan is a professional woman in her own right and that she is making a significant contribution to the war effort – a little 'rich' coming from Moira, but nevertheless it put the woman in her place. Whilst she, Moira, can criticise would-be family members, she sees criticism from others – now that she has acknowledged her son's engagement – as a personal slight.

Moira is pleased to hear that the Coopers will eventually move to a larger and presumably better house when the opportunity arises; hopefully before the war comes to an end.

Both parties agree that as soon as Mr Harry Cooper arrives home on leave, his permission will be sought and a wedding date fixed as far as that is possible, given the present circumstances.

Settling on a date is proving more and more difficult. Harry is due home in a fortnight, but James has now been asked to report in a few days' time to the Artists' Rifles training depot in London, which fortunately is not too far away.

A week later he attends an interview at the Old Drill Hall near Euston Station before being sent to No. 15 Officers' Training Battalion at Hare Hall, Romford in Essex. This is followed by a spell of training at the Officers' School, Tidworth.

On his return Susan enquires, 'What was it like? Did you miss me?'

'Of course I missed you. Most of the time was spent tramping across muddy fields, digging trenches, learning about bomb throwing, map reading, first aid (you'd love that), firing rifles and machine guns, amongst other things.'

'But you don't need to know all that if you are flying an aeroplane.'

'The pilot still has to navigate so reading a map is essential, and aeroplanes are fitted with machine guns. Most of the chaps are going into the infantry and this training is essential. I'm glad I'll be flying as I don't really enjoy the route marches.'

'When do you start flying?'

'After I've spent a few days training at St Omer.'

'Where's that?'

'It's in France. The idea is to give us some notion of what it's like over there, and the RFC's HQ is based there so I'll be able to get a look at what I might be flying. It's really exciting. It'll certainly be a change from listening to lectures by some of the old duffers – Colonels and Brigadiers. They seem happier to talk about the Boer War; one even chuntered on about the war in the Crimea. After that I go to Biggin Hill to learn to fly – I can't wait.'

Susan mentally recalls the damaged state of the patients at the military hospital in Canterbury and shudders at the thought of what might happen to James. However, she believes it expedient not to relay her thoughts, or to explain what injuries he may incur.

'But before all that, you know you must meet my dad and ask for my delicate hand in marriage.'

'This I swear to do my sweet and at the earliest opportunity.'

CHAPTER FIFTEEN

It is a relief for Harry to be away from the dangers of the Front Line. Bombardment from the enemy at this time is sporadic rather than continuous, but that is not to say the shells that land are any less lethal. The company is feeling more relaxed, particularly as they know that the next destination will be Boulogne and then Folkestone. The danger now being, Captain East reminds his NCOs, that the men might become less focused and therefore too relaxed, loose concentration and hence take unnecessary risks.

In the interim they are tasked with assisting the Royal Engineers with stacking, and then moving large quantities of trench-bound equipment. Such is the size of the stores depot that it is an obvious target for the enemy aircraft and long range guns. Harry Cooper has obtained a second stripe, and as a Corporal he is in-charge of a section which today is tasked with preparing materials and equipment for troops in the Front-Line. A runner has arrived with a requisition order for duckboards, barbed wire, hurdles, entrenching tools, plus lengths of timber of a specific length. The timber is stored in a barn on the edge of the logistics area. Harry, ensconced in the attic of the barn, is measuring the required lengths of timber and, to save time and effort, is heaving them out of the gap in the wall – which at one time was a window – to the boys below for carrying to the motorised transport. Suddenly he is almost deafened by a loud blast. A shell has exploded next to the barn.

His reaction is immediate. He jumps to the ground and runs for safety to the basement of the main building. A man runs towards him. It’s his cousin George and he’s shouting something.

‘I can’t bloody hear you. What are you saying?’

George comes closer and making a megaphone with his hands shouts, 'I thought you would be in bits. Christ that was close! Are you OK?'

'I will be when the bloody ringing in my ears stops.'

The two men return to inspect the damage and find the nose-cap of the shell buried alongside the barn. They go to inform Sergeant Boneaply who has also heard the explosion and is wondering if anyone is hurt. Harry is still quite shaken and is advised to rest before carrying on.

It is clear that the enemy has, as a result of the illumination provided by the barn which is now on fire, discovered the cache of stores. A squadron of enemy bombers believed to be Taubes, comes flying over, and using the barn as a marker, discharge more bombs. The raid lasts some considerable time as the planes make several passes. The artillery's guns are firing in retaliation, while Sergeant Boneaply, Corporal Harry Cooper, George Smith and others take refuge in the cellar of the farmhouse.

They have now been joined by Corporal Mossey who shakes his fists and shouts at the enemy pilots, 'I don't want to die now you bastards, not before I see my new baby.'

'Can we run for it Sergeant,' asks a fresh faced youth.

‘Where are we going to run to? You bloody numpty! There will be no running or moving until we receive orders to do so’, barks the Sergeant.

An hour and half later the men clamber from their protective hideaways and inspect the damage. Parts of the stores depot are flattened, shafts and splinters of wood are strewn across the yard, roofing tiles now form piles in dishevelled heaps, and the barn - where Harry was throwing timber down from the upstairs floor - is reduced to a mound of rubble. What can be salvaged will have to be moved to a safer location.

‘Corporal Cooper, Corporal Mossey over here’, shouts Sergeant Boney. I want you two to scout round the area and check for human damage, and make a list of those who are still standing. Then report back to me. Now go.’

Fortunately there are no fatalities, just a couple of broken limbs where masonry has landed on those unable to take cover quickly enough. One old lag known as ‘Ciggie’ on account of his ability to do almost anything, including eating while holding a cigarette butt in his mouth, appears to have damaged his ankle and is limping about and looking in pain; he appears to be in no fit state to continue carrying stores.

‘Typical,’ says Mossey. ‘Look at him, can’t wait until it’s his turn to get on the train to go home. He has to try and work a flanker and get off early.’

‘Well, it’s Sunday in’ it, a day of rest’ retorts Ciggie.

‘Oh, very droll’ replies Harry. ‘Come on old son. Let’s get you off the playing field, time for an early bath and onto the train home.’

‘Before we go, have you got a ciggie? I can’t move on a leg like this without a smoke, can I?’

Everyone hopes that the shelling last night will do them a favour and that they will be accompanying Ciggie, and hence hop on the train to Boulogne sooner than expected.

‘Of course you realise Ciggie that you may have to stay here longer than anticipated because of your bad leg’, says Harry.

‘What do you mean?’

‘Well, if it’s broken they’ll have to patch you up properly, and you may have to be confined to bed for a week or two while it heals.’

Ciggie looks horrified. ‘They can’t bleedin-well do that to me,’ he shouts. ‘I got to get home, see me missus, see me kids, have a couple of pints.’ Where upon he stands up and takes a step or two.

‘Would you Adam n’Eve it’, comments Corporal Harry Cooper. ‘He’s cured. He’s walking about unaided; a ruddy miracle. You’ve been caught out this time. That’ll cost you a whole packet of ciggies, lad.’

‘You bugger, Corporal Cooper.’

At this point Lieutenant Laurence Griffiths comes into sight. The look on his face suggests there is a problem and they think of the worst scenario. They expect to be told to move back to where they had come from and re-join the Line. ‘Well chaps I’m afraid I’ve some relatively bad news’. There follows a communal groan. ‘But don’t panic, we are not going back to the trenches.’ There is a unanimous sigh of relief. ‘The problem, I’m told, concerns the railway. The Hun has damaged the track and the railway line is *kaput.* Which means we have two choices: we either wait here until it is repaired or we march to Boulogne which is to be?’

‘We don’t care how far it is’, they chorus.

‘Right, I hoped you’d say that, because the rest of the company is already formed up on the road. So, shall we join them?’

They could not move fast enough. Even Sergeant Boneaply is moving at the double, Ciggie has re-discovered how to run and within two minutes they have collected their kit and formed fours. Captain Peter East takes his place at the head of the company column and gives the order: 'By the Left, to Boulogne and home, Quick March.'

To the sound of *It's a Long way to Tipperary* and *We're Here because we're Here*, and other ditties including, what has now become the Harry's song, *If You Were the Only Girl in the World,* the company warbles and cheers its way along the flat lands of Belgium, and across the French frontier to the port of Boulogne. As they cross the frontier they break into, *There's a long, long trail a–winding, into the land of my dreams …*'

It takes the best part of a day to reach their destination. Nevertheless, the thought of Blighty and home keeps them going. On arrival at the docks the Kent Company's jollity is tempered by the sight of serried lines of stretcher cases set out on the quayside awaiting boarding. Clearly some of the patients have lost limbs, others, being swathed in bandages, are in need of serious surgery due to having suffered burns and other complicated injuries. The remaining Kent boys who had made it could not help but be immensely grateful that they had arrived in one piece. They'll keep my Susan in work thinks Harry.

The crossing is, thankfully, smoother than Harry's outward journey. On arrival at Folkestone the incapacitated take precedence and so it is a couple of hours before Harry's company disembark. His cousin George has made contact and they settle down in the carriage heading north along the coastline towards the Isle of Thanet and beyond. The singing has stopped and the boys take the opportunity to sleep or contemplate the welcome they'll receive when they get home. Harry and George alight at Westgate station. George heads into the town. Harry keeps on walking past the edge of the conurbation towards the countryside.

Harry stands at the top of the hill and listens. He is listening to the silence, broken only by the singing of a nightingale. The absence of gun fire, explosions and the smell of cordite and death is refreshing and tangible. He inhales deeply in an effort to cleanse his senses of the stench of war, and pauses temporarily before proceeding down the hill to his front door. He could walk straight in but he knocks first and waits; he wants to see the surprised look of delight on Beryl's face. It's Sunday evening so he knows she will be at home but she doesn't know the exact time of his arrival. He imagines how she will be flitting around the house, tidying things, her blond hair tousled and her cheeks red from the effort. Susan, will not be home until the morning as she is working the late-shift at the hospital. She had wanted to take the day off but James had persuaded her to allow her parents some little time together first; besides, he argues, 'If we were married, wouldn't you want to be the first to meet me?'

On answering the knock on the door Harry kisses his wife on the lips, but keeps her at arm's length. He moves quickly past her and into the lean-to at the side of the house. Once there he begins to strip off his uniform and toss the garments into the copper boiler, explaining to Beryl that they are not only sweaty but covered in lice. They need washing, as does he. Minutes later he stands by the dining table denuded of his clothes. 'So, now you've got your kit off, what do we do now?' asks Beryl. Harry grins expectantly.

Susan arrives home in the morning. She can't wait to see her dad. She rushes down the hill, and bursts through the front door. Her mother is sitting at the dining table drinking tea.

'Well, is he here, is he here?' she asks with excitement.

'Yes, of course he is.'

'So, where is he?

'He's in bed. He's tired.'

'Yes, I bet he is. Have you exhausted him?'

'I beg your pardon young lady, cheeky minx! He's been fighting in a war, that's why he's knackered.'

'Can I see him?'

‘Of course you can. Here, take his tea up to him.’

The sounds of joy at father and daughter’s reunion echo around the house. Eventually Susan descends the stairs and explains to her mother – as if she didn’t know – how good it is to have her dad home.

‘Did he tell you what it was like?’ asks Beryl.

‘I didn’t have a chance’ says Harry, appearing at the kitchen door. ‘We need her at the Front; she could talk the enemy to death. Oh, and I have been informed that I will be meeting the marvellous James later today. But I’m not sure where?’

‘Here, dad, here, and then we’ll have something to eat.’

‘No. I think I should meet him on neutral ground. I don’t want to inhibit the boy and I don’t want you two looking over my shoulder. I’d like to chat to him – man to man – and get to know him. I suggest, Susan, you bring him to the pub, introduce us and then leave. We’ll make our way here when we have become better acquainted.’

‘That sounds a bit serious and formal. You’re not going to give him a lecture, are you Harry?’ inquires Beryl.

‘Or get him drunk’, adds Susan.

'No, of course not, this will be the first meeting. The second one will be with his parents. I'll probably need his advice so that I don't make any social gaffs when going to their 'ouse.'

'My, you think of everything, don't yer. You make it sound like a military operation. Have you been spending your time planning this out?' asks Beryl.

'Well … I've had plenty of time. Believe it or not there isn't much else to do between the fighting. You sort out the time Susan and tell me when to be there, and find out what he likes to drink. On second thoughts, I expect you already know that.'

After lunch Susan goes to meet James and excitedly tells him of the plan. 'Are you going to be in uniform?' she enquires. 'No, I think it best if we meet, as your dad says, on neutral ground and in neutral attire.'

'They say that an officer or a potential officer is still distinguishable when in mufti' says Susan, laughing.

'I will not be wearing a bowler hat or carrying a rolled umbrella, if that is what you're hinting at', retorts James.

Susan, having made the arrangement, dashes home to inform her dad of the timing, and the pub – the smartest in town – where they will meet.

‘Hurry up dad, come on!’ urges Susan.

‘Yes, alright … anybody would think I was meeting the Prince of Wales.’

‘Don’t be silly dad, James is much more important.’

James is seated in a quiet corner of the snug when Susan and Harry arrive. He rises, proffers his hand to Harry and says, ‘A pleasure to meet you, Sir.’

‘It’s good to meet you at last James. But let’s dispense with the ‘Sir’, we’re not in the Army now.’ James respectfully addresses him as Mr Cooper, this is acceptable to Harry. In fact he rather likes the polite deference shown by James. It takes some time before they can prise Susan out of the door of the pub. Initially they talk of things military and of family, before James plucks up the courage to ask the inevitable question. Harry replies that it is obvious to him that his daughter is in love, ‘some might say besotted’ and that he can see no reason for objecting to their becoming engaged, provided his parents are in agreement, which, of course, they are.

Later in the week Harry and Beryl are invited to Gordon and Moira’s house so that all prospective in-laws can be formally introduced. They laugh about the initial meeting in the basement during the air raid and all agree that in the end it saved time. Susan and James want to get married straight away, but Harry only has a couple more days leave left and it is decided to postpone the wedding until after the banns have been read in church; Moira thinks this the right and proper way of doing things.

Beryl and Susan, along with James, go to the station to bid Harry good-bye. Conversation is a little strained; it's never easy saying goodbye at such a time. 'We may meet in different circumstances and in a different country next time', remarks Harry. 'I hope we do Mr Cooper, best of luck' replies James. Harry embraces his wife and daughter who are desperately trying to hold back the tears, but plainly failing. He boards the train and departs, hopefully to return again, alive and in one piece.

CHAPTER SIXTEEN

It is not long before Susan is again bidding 'farewell' to someone, this time it's James. She doesn't accompany him to the station as she is on duty, and, anyway, he won't be that far away so they expect to see each other fairly soon. He is accompanied to the station by his parents.

His stay at Reading is brief as he is soon posted to Biggin Hill where he studies all things aeronautical. James feels immediately at home, although he is a little taken aback by the intensity of training. He passes through the usual progression of engine-fitting, rigging, machine-gunnery before graduating from the Sopwith Pup to the S.E.5 aeroplane. He only has nine hours of flying and two hours of practical tuition when the instructor decides to leave the two-seater bi-plane in sole command of 2nd Lieutenant James Hemmings. The rookie pilot is clad in wool-lined flying boots, flying helmet and goggles and looks every bit like the flying ace. Lessons in aerobatics and formation flying follow. His enthusiasm, prior theoretical knowledge and his technical ability reflect the relatively short period it takes before he is given sole control of the aircraft. These periods of captaincy became more and more extended. Training is being rushed as it is post Battle of the Somme and the Army is in desperate need of pilots.

The repeated formula – 'Switch on. Suck in. Contact' – becomes second nature; each time the air mechanic swings the prop and the engine fires James feels the adrenaline start to pump. 'Chocks away' call the ground crew and he taxis into position, engages the throttle, revs the engine and takes off. Up into the sky and cruising over the verdant fields: bliss thinks James.

The most dangerous part is the landing; getting the two front wheels and the small tail wheel to touch down at the same time is difficult, especially when trying to negotiate a stiff cross wind. Eventually, following several solos flights, which include completing two figure of eight courses, 2nd Lieutenant James Hemmings graduates as a fully-qualified pilot with the Royal Flying Corps.

James is so pleased and proud to be awarded his 'wings'. Apart from indulging in his passion, he is in an environment which allows him to enjoy himself with his peers. Until now his life has been centred on home and work in a factory with women – not that he disliked the factory girls. Of course he misses his fiancée, but here he is with young men of comparable age, and he is having fun. It is true, there is the odd accident but he is not involved and the exuberance of youth ensures that he and his flying colleagues soon overcome these setbacks.

While he is with the squadron he indulges in the cunning game that the pilots play on the spectators who come to the airfield on Sundays to watch the flying. The fliers conceal a dummy dressed in a flying suit in the two-seater aircraft and after a loop over the airfield the accompanying observer ejects the dummy, then squats low so as not to be visible. A waiting ambulance concealing an officer suitably clad, rushes to the scene and he swaps places with the dummy. The plane lands with only the pilot's head visible to the spectators. The reaction of the spectators is one of expectant horror until all is revealed – a boyish but not very tasteful prank. Susan, when she hears about it, responds with an attitude that can best be described as unamused. She thinks it particularly unfair to those who may have lost relatives who were pilots.

She is better pleased when he gets posted to Dover. The occasional party in the officers' mess is enjoyable, they are exuberant affairs with much singing, dancing and imbibing; there is nothing like that at the hospital. Within a further fortnight James has completed his training in the different types of aircraft.

This boosts his confidence and he appears a trifle egotistical, not to say a little arrogant and pompous, as the pilots feel somewhat superior to the infantry subalterns. This is in part due to the fact that they can be seen to be in action when they chase the occasional Zeppelin across the Channel, whereas the infantryman does his fighting abroad, un-witnessed by those at home. The reality of flying missions over hostile country is yet to be experienced.

His mother wants a family photograph. On the day the photographer arrives James manages to persuade the photographer to take an additional copy of himself alone, which he gives to Susan. Everyone agrees he looks resplendent in his double-breasted tunic, colloquially known as a 'maternity jacket', Sam Browne belt, cavalry breeches, brown field riding boots, forage cap, and with his newly acquired 'wings' displayed on his tunic. His mother insists that his father purchase their son's military accoutrements from the best tailors.

CHAPTER SEVENTEEN

'Why are we carrying our large packs as well?' enquires Ciggie as the platoon prepares for the forthcoming action in the battlefield of mud.

'You want to eat, don't yer?' replies Sergeant Boney.'

'Yeah, but I ain't a bleedin' camel, and this ain't the desert; unless you call them water-filled bomb craters oases.' 'For once, Ciggie, you've asked a very pertinent question.' The Sergeant raises his voice so that everyone can hear. 'And the answer is, it will be impossible for supplies to be sent up to us. That is until we have secured the high ground and established a proper defensive position and constructed a communication trench. This also means every man will be carrying extra rations, more ammunition, and a spade or an entrenching tool.'

'Corporal Cooper will be alright. I heard he got a lot of practice while he was on leave, digging the back garden,' jokes his cousin George.

‘Yep, but at least I went indoors when it was raining, and when I wanted something to eat.’

‘That wife of yours spoils you, or is it your daughter who cooks your dinner?’

‘It wasn’t Susan. I hardly ever saw her. She was too busy with her fiancée.’

‘When are they getting married then?’

‘When he comes home from France and I come home from Belgium. And, yeah, it could be a long, bloody wait.’

‘Oh, and by the way Ciggie,’ says Sergeant Boneaply with a degree of vocal relish, ‘you’re our rifle-grenadier, which means you have another haversack with six grenades to carry. That should balance things up.’ In response Ciggie loudly lets rip with all the swear words he can possible muster, and then repeats them for good measure.

Captain East addresses the company. ‘I know it’s muddy and difficult but we’ve got to keep in an extended line as we will be following a creeping barrage. This will continue for several minutes only a hundred yards in front. It is of the utmost importance that we keep as close to our barrage as possible.’

‘Jesus, I hope the gunners know what they’re doing? And they’d better be fucking accurate!’ Sentiments voiced by George Smith and echoed by every man in the trench.

At midnight they crawl into their individual placements in the damp earth and attempt to sleep. Harry thinks of home, of Beryl and Susan and hopes he’ll see his daughter get married. After what seems to be an inordinately short time, Harry is jabbed in the ribs by a fellow junior NCO, Corporal Mossy. ‘Time to move old son, better get a grip of your blokes’, he whispers. Dawn is breaking and all along the line spectre-like figures emerge as one from the earthen holes; the silence is interrupted by mutterings and the *click! click! click!* of men snapping bayonets onto their rifles.

‘This is your three minute call,’ announces Lieutenant Griffiths.

‘God, he thinks he’s conducting a bloody show,’ comments Harry, who knows a little bit about performing on stage.

‘Well he is, ain’t he: plenty rehearsals, heightened nervous tension, loads of adrenalin, curtain up and over the top – same bloody thing innit!’ comments Ciggie. He has an uncanny way of capturing a moment in a few choice words or phrase.

‘Beginners on stage,’ calls the platoon commander.

Now everyone is quiet, taut, tense and ready to perform. Several mouth words of prayer, a couple cross themselves, Sergeant Boneaply stands stiff and erect, his eyes harden, Ciggie grips his rifle until his knuckles turn white, the youngest lad is visibly shaking, Corporal Mossey kisses the photo of his new baby and replaces it carefully into a top pocket, while Harry tries to put his mind in neutral: each has his own way of trying to cope with the tension of the moment.

Captain East blows the dreaded whistle and like automatons men clamber up the wooden ladders, into the open and spread out in an extended line. All credit to the artillery, they have started the barrage on time. Officers attempt to shout orders but the noise from the guns is deafening; it's difficult to follow instructions. The only thing to do is to keep an eye on the man either side, keep in line and move forward together.

Blinding flashes from behind, now in front light up the night sky and then vanish. The thunderous noise from the guns and the landing of the murderously exploding shells magnify the mayhem.

The thick, glutinous mud is more and more difficult to walk through, boots become caked and heavy. The additional weight of ammunition and equipment makes progress painfully slow. The barrage stops suddenly when the company has reached half-way across the salient. There follows a brief lull before the enemy, now repositioned on their entrenched ramparts, open up with a fusillade of machine gun fire. Men begin to fall like ninepins.

The stretcher bearers, what is left of them, are making heroic attempts to get about the battlefield as quickly as possible. The wounded try to mark their places in the hope of being rescued by sticking their bayonets into the muddy ground with rifle butts pointing skywards. Like a forest of skittles they are knocked down by bursts from enemy machine guns.

Remarkably men follow in the manner of well-herded sheep, no one looks back. But the organised line begins to break. Deep shell holes are impassable as troops pick their way forward; their bodies crouched in an attempt to lessen the target and as a result of the weight being carried. Harry leads his section on a detour in an effort to get to higher ground. Ciggie is at the rear of the section and starting to fall behind, no doubt hindered by the extra weight of the grenades he is carrying. He is also handicapped by being shorter than average and with every step he is sinking up to his knees.

Harry finds himself in a shell hole along with his section. He has difficulty trying to move. A stinging pain in his right thigh means he is immobile and George takes charge of the section; they move forward without Harry. He has no choice but to stay where he is until it's safe to try and crawl back to his line, or be rescued by stretcher bearers – if they are still operating. He is now an observer in the carnage.

The glutinous mud can be his saviour. A shell lands close to Harry's left and is buried, the viscous clay cushions the effect and decreases its killing power. The enemy snipers are proving more effective. One man, clearly out of his mind, staggers around for several seconds before his helmet is flipped into the air and he falls like a sawn-off log. His body tumbles into the crater. Harry stares in horror at the immobile body. The profile of his face showing, eyes staring and a stub of a cigarette is stuck to his bottom lip. It's Ciggie. His body starts to palpitate, his face changes colour, to puce, and then purple, eyes dilate, before turning a shade of grey: the company's clown, the young court jester is no more. Everyone will feel the loss.

Several hours of ceaseless sniping come to an end when a penetrative wet mist descends over the killing ground making visibility difficult, thankfully. Harry takes this opportunity to slowly and painfully drag himself back to his lines.

An hour later Harry manages to reach the trench he'd vacated earlier in the day and rolls over the top of the parapet. He is helped down onto the fire step. Stretcher bearers are called and he is carried to the first aid post. Sometime later George arrives and sits by his side. 'Thank God you're still alive. I thought you'd bought it or worse still', jokingly adding, 'a bloody General Staff officer could have been injured!'

'Its worse' interjects Harry, 'Ciggie has had his ciggie stubbed out for the last time.'

'Christ, No!'

No more is needed to be said as Harry is carried the short journey down the communication trench to the dressing station, thence to a Casualty Clearing Station by ambulance. The convoy of ambulances shake and rattle their way down pitted roads to the base hospital, every jolt, every bump sending sharp pains shooting down his leg. Harry isn't sure whether his wound will be classified as a 'Blighty one', or worse still, end in an amputation. The sooner he reaches the medical centre the quicker the injury can be cleaned, and the less chance of gangrene setting-in. At the very least he will receive some respite from the rain, the mud, the guns and death: for this he is unspeakably grateful.

Harry's company is moved back to Base Camp during which time Captain East and Sergeant Boneaply take the opportunity to count the losses and visit those who are injured.

'Good morning Corporal Cooper' says Captain East.

‘Excuse me sir,’ interjects Boney. ‘Don’t you mean Sergeant Cooper?’

‘Oh, so I do. Congratulations.’

‘What have I done to deserve this?’

‘Alas, we have had to make a few changes after that last push. First, the bad news, you’ll be getting a new platoon commander. Lieutenant Laurence Griffiths bought it, and, yes, we heard the additional sad news about Ciggie. But the good news, if I can put it that way, is that Sergeant Boneaply – now Sergeant-major has been promoted and you are the platoon sergeant.’

‘And there’s further good news’ adds the new Sergeant-major. ‘You will be going away for a week on a senior NCO course, once you are up an about. Although it may be in lieu of any sick leave you may be entitled to, but the course is in Blighty.’

‘Well, I knew there’d be a catch. I’m sorry to hear about Lieutenant Griffiths. He was a good bloke and well-liked. So, do you know when I might go on this course?’

‘I think that depends on your recovery. I hope it is quick. Goodbye, Sergeant.’

‘Thank you, sirs.’

Much to his surprise and delight Harry is put on a train to the nearest hospital. This hospital bed is much more comfortable than the cot in the medical station, food is better and they even provide note paper and a pencil, so he is able to catch up on his letter writing. Beryl duly receives a missive from the Front, it reads:

‘To the only girl in the world, you won’t believe it but I’m sat in a nice comfy bed with white sheets and a cup of tea, not as nice as your tea, of course. There are beautiful girls running around serving me. As you might have guessed, I’m in hospital. I’m not in a desperate state – I can still walk with the aid of a crutch. But hopefully I’ll get rid of that soon. Tell Dolly, George is OK. But sadly we lost the funny young bloke I told you about, Ciggie, and our platoon officer amongst others. I hope you are keeping well and no doubt our daughter is pining for her James. Who knows, if I get some leave we may be able to attend a wedding! But as our ex-officer and actor would have said, ‘There’s a long, long trail a-winding, into the land of my dreams’ and to you.
Take care, your loving husband. Harry.

There is an additional and unexpected bonus for those admitted to hospital. It takes the form of entertainments, and it’s not the usual ad hoc and at times very crude in-house amusements. This is a professional concert party. A cast of six artistes dressed in colourful costumes enter onto the stage in the YMCA hut. The burst of colour and the music raises the spirits. Harry wished Lieutenant Laurence Griffiths was still here – he would have been in his element. And Ciggie would have remembered all the topical jokes, added a military twist to them and regaled the lads back in the line following the show.

All the old favourites are sung. The soldiers give voice to the chorus with gusto, and when what has become Harry's family signature tune – *If you were the only girl in the world* - he sings as best he can, until he cannot help but shed a few quiet tears. The culmination of the show is indicated by the cast boarding a cardboard cut-out of a ship while singing the ubiquitous favourite, *Take Me Back to Dear Old Blighty.* The response is loud and tumultuous. Harry wonders when it will be his turn to board the troop ship back across the Channel and home, and possibly take his girls to a show.

CHAPTER EIGHTEEN

James has bid farewell to his pals at Manston and now faces the unenviable task of saying goodbye to the family and Susan.

The autumn leaves blow haphazardly along the station platform, sometimes this way sometimes that before forming spiralling eddies at opposite ends of the station. It seems like a metaphor for life: no one knows where they are going or where they will end up. The possibility of James meeting his future father in law is like the windswept debris, each travelling in different directions. 'Will the families ever get together and will he ever get married?'

James is attempting to be nonchalant, but he is beginning to worry as the realization of not seeing his loved ones for several months becomes apparent. He hurries to get aboard the train, and swallows hard before leaning out of the window for a last embrace with Susan. 'Take care my love', she cries. Feelings of melancholy and sadness multiply as the rhythmical clank of the wheels on the rails diminish into the distance. Moira and Susan cling to each other for as long as possible, their emotions now unrestrained. Gordon leaves his arm extended in the air until he is sure James can no longer see them.

It is not a long journey to Folkestone. Like Harry and hundreds of thousands before him he deposits himself and his kit on the troop ship. Lines of soldiers lean on the ship's rails watching in silence as the harbour disappears in the distance. 'Well, what do you think?' asks the fellow newly qualified pilot, and member of the Royal Flying Corps. 'To be honest, I'm not sure. Half of me is excited the other half dejected; I've just said goodbye to my fiancée. What about you?'

‘Oh, I’m excited too but … only … only I can’t help feeling a bit scared, particularly having seen all those wounded chaps being loaded onto the in-bound trains.’

‘We’ll be alright Gerald, I’m sure of it.’ Replies James with an air of forced bravado, designed to boost his own as well as Gerald’s confidence, adding ‘next stop France.’

‘And so to the Front,’ gulps Gerald.

The Army offices in Boulogne appear to James to be the epitome of the War Office he once had the misfortune of visiting; a centre for uniformed marionettes, a place where the administrative clerks pass you from one office to another prior to providing you with information required, which, as it turns out, could have been obtained at the start.

On entrance to the ‘sorting office’ the senior staff officers, as expected, are whisked off individually in chauffeur driven cars. Officers of field rank share what army ‘taxis’ there are and disappear. Then company and regimental personnel form up in their groups and entrain, and are shunted off to their destinations. The remainder, the ‘odd bods’, are herded into a miscellaneous group and wait around until some middle ranking officer makes a decision; in James’ case it is the wrong one as he is directed towards a train bound for Etaples. Fortunately he realises that this is for those heading to the military hospital and the prison, and manages to disembark as the train begins to move out of the station.

The transport officer, now free of the initial rush and confusion, points James in the direction of the pilots pool. James is not encouraged by the reports elicited from other airman, some of whom had been through this process before. The latter take it calmly and are content to sit in a bar in the evening. James and other newly commissioned fliers are eager to get to a squadron. A fellow pilot returning from the office tells James that the list of personnel is in a muddle. 'The single-seater aviators are mixed up with duel-seated heavy bomber people,' he says. There is no flying in this area and the noise from the heavy guns rarely audible. This is not what James wants: he is naïve enough to want to go straight into action.

Early next day James returns to the office. He is dismayed by the number of officers hanging about, some veterans, some new; they are giving their details to the clerks for entering on the list. James wanders into the orderly room, discovers that the officer in-charge is at breakfast, and so takes a surreptitious look at the two-page list of pilots only to find that his name is near the bottom.

'I say Corporal, I do think my name ought to be higher up the list than that, after all, I've been here over a week,' James says with tongue in cheek.

'Unfortunately the original list was mislaid and this temporary one collated rather hurriedly, sir. We are trying to get those who have been waiting the longest off first. I'm about to compile a more up to date list. I'll put you near the top as you have been waiting so long; if that's OK with you, sir?'

'That will be fine. Thank you kindly, Corporal.'

Later that day James and three other pilots get a lift in a Crossley tender lorry, the sort adapted with a canvas cover for carrying supplies. The pilots sit facing each other in the back. Not the most comfortable ride, but no matter, it is transport to the designated encampments.

The young pilots exhibit the exuberance of youth, the driver, on the other hand, appears to be a dour creature. Any attempts to engage him in conversation and possibly elicit some information as to their destination, results in monosyllabic responses. Either he doesn't like speaking to young officers or he just thinks them ignorant and foolish. The truck speeds along the chalk-lined dusty winding road, past damaged and discarded military vehicles and onwards through war-torn villages.

James recalls his brief introduction at St Omer nine months previously. But this is different, this is not a training exercise, soon he will be up there in the sky and in combat. Pilots are dropped off at different points until eventually only James is left bouncing around in the back of the truck.

The driver turns the vehicle off the main track and bumps along via a small track through a copse into a wide expanse of open field. In the distance parked in a neat line, are the aircraft and to the right stand wooden huts, a large tented marquee and an assortment of parked vehicles. The windsock is struggling to stay horizontal.

James jumps down from the tailboard, makes an attempt to get his kit when an orderly arrives to assist him and carries his kitbag and valise. The driver now speaks in staccato sentences. ‘This is your final destination, sir.’ He then ticks James’ name off his list. ‘This is number 40 Squadron RFC. Name of place: Trezennes.’ James thanks him for the information but is a little concerned by the way the driver emphasised the words, ‘final destination’.

A short walk through a scraggy orchard towards the officers’ billet with surrounding bell-tents and James arrives at the squadron office. This is next to the Mess hut with its veranda, which looks pleasant enough, rather like a village cricket pavilion. His kit is deposited by the front door.

Meeting colleagues, especially as the new boy, is always a bit nerve-racking and James hopes that there will be a recognisable face inside. As he is about to knock on the door of the office he hears someone call his name.

'James. Good to see you. That's a bit of luck, you coming here. No point in going into the office, the C.O. is out at present. Come into the Mess and have a cup of tea or a drink.' This is just what James needs, a familiar face. It is John Bentley, whom he met when on a course at Dover. 'What about my kit, askes James?' 'Don't worry about that an orderly will take it to your room'. On entry to the Mess he is introduced to a couple of the pilots who are lounging in armchairs, smoking and chatting.

'I say, you are very lucky to be here James. Do you know who our commanding officer is?' He doesn't wait for a reply. 'It's no less than Major Robert Loraine MC, the noted West End actor.'

'Really!'

'Yes, really, and what is more, did you know that George Bernard Shaw is his god-father?'

'No I didn't. So?'

'So GBS, who is reputed to disapprove of the war, is visiting the Front – care of the Government – and what is more, he's coming here to see the C.O. What do you think of that? And that's not all. We, but not the C.O, are to perform his one-act play, O'Flaherty VC. We had lots of practice – or should I say rehearsal. What do you think of that?'

'I'm impressed. Are you in it and what's it about?'

'No, I'm just helping back stage. I think it's a bit controversial as the O'Flaherty VC character disagrees with the war but sees it as a means of escape from home and joins up, and becomes a hero. He returns home but is restless and cannot stand the arguing civilians and returns to the Front. At least that's what I understand it to be about.'

'Sounds fairly accurate to me.'

'And what is more, it is the first time it has been performed, so this is a world premiere.'

'Fascinating; I look forward to seeing it. When is it to be performed?'

'In the marquee … this very evening.'

James is pleased to have met a friend and is impressed with the social activities although he realises that this is probably exceptional, given the honoured guest. The next hour or so is spent being introduced to other members of the squadron while waiting to see the C.O. He also has time to view the

German propeller affixed to the wall under which are painted the names of squadron personnel who have been decorated for bravery. It is an imposing list and to a new pilot: and an intimidating one.

The adjutant, Captain Court, is an old soldier sporting Boer War ribbons above his left breast pocket. He has a kind face and a first-rate bushy moustache, one any general would be proud to display. He calls James into the office, takes down his particulars and instructs him to be ready to report immediately to the C.O. when called. However, he feels it necessary to warn him that Major Loraine does not tolerate undisciplined officers, either on the ground or in the air. He then proceeds to tell him the Major was awarded the MC in 1915. Prior to the war he was famous for becoming the first aviator ever to fly to the Isle Wight and later to fly from Ireland to England. The adjutant also adds that the C.O. was the initiator of the aeronautical term 'joystick', indicating that he has a sense of humour. He had also commanded the squadron during the horrendous Battle of the Somme.

It is with some trepidation that James waits to be summoned to meet this living hero. He doesn't have to wait long.

James notes that the C.O. is tall with a trim moustache and broad shoulders; he looks every inch the star actor and the famous aviator, which is what he is. He waves to James to sit down. 'I'm used to things going like clockwork: experience has taught me that rehearsal is never wasted.' The usual perfunctory questions are then quickly run through. James scores some brownie-points by having served with the Dover squadron, meaning he is not straight from a flying school. Nevertheless, he will have to take a preliminary flight before engaging with the enemy.

George Bernard Shaw arrives that evening and is accompanied by Major Loraine MC throughout his short visit. The playwright stays to see his play before being driven back to the Army HQ. But quite what GBS thinks of the production is not known to James. The young pilot is finding his way around, and being shy fails to take the opportunity to speak to the famous dramatist.

Morning comes and James stands expectantly outside the C.O's office. He is feeling a little apprehensive but ready for his inaugural flight over enemy territory. To his disappointment he spends the next three-quarters of an hour in a tutorial with the second in-command. Part one is a navigation lesson; it concerns the geography of this part of France with particular reference to allied and enemy defensive positions, and areas of particular danger. Part two of the briefing is about formation flying and the techniques used when facing the enemy in a one-to-one situation. After a break he is to put some of this newly-acquired knowledge into practice.

The flight takes place in a two-seater. James is not the pilot. He acts as the observer. In this case he is viewing and identifying the enemy positions. A second trip is where he operates a camera and another is taken where his flying skills are assessed. 'How do you feel' asks the instructor. 'A trifle nervous, is the CO watching?' 'No, he's had to go away to Division HQ; you've just got me to contend with. I'll be writing your report … Don't worry, you appear to be more knowledgeable than most of the red-arsed pilots we get.' Most of the flight is over friendly terrain or high enough to be out of range of enemy fire. The three flights prove very useful and James is grateful for this introduction. Without this reconnaissance exercise he would doubtlessly have got lost. He is reminded that Major Loraine is a hard task-master and that he is not very tolerant of young cavalier pilots who don't do their homework and make, what he considers, to be avoidable mistakes.

James is now adjudged to be ready for combat. Next time he will expect to make contact with the enemy.

CHAPTER NINETEEN

Dolly Smith places her overall and cotton bobble hat into her bag for washing at home and having divested herself of the brown factory uniform, makes for the exit. She is the first to leave the factory. When crossing the yard she hears an explosion. Ignoring the sound, she hurries to the exit unaware of the catastrophe occurring above her head. An enemy plane has been hit and is on fire and heading downwards towards the yard. It explodes in mid-air and fragments of metal are scattered over a wide area.

The factory hooter sounds loudly, workers begin to hurriedly make for the exits from the various buildings. Mr Woods, the foreman, quickly organises people into groups to fetch buckets to convey water from the dykes to put out the fragmented fires. It is imperative to stop the fires spreading, and igniting the stacked cotton waste stored next to the shed that contains explosive material.

Gordon Hemmings is on the phone to the local fire brigade, making contact with other factory managers nearby; they immediately respond by dispatching water-pumps and other items of firefighting equipment. He also phones the local hospital for an ambulance: at this stage no one knows the number of people injured, if any.

Susan has just arrived to meet her mother and watches transfixed as the plane explodes. She has no idea if it is a British or Germany machine; her thoughts are immediately of James. About to enter the gates she notices a motionless body lying prostrate. She hurries to the inert frame in order to administer first aid. It is female. There is no answer to her calls as she nears the woman whose face is buried in the grass. A gentle shake elicits no response, she turns the figure over and to her horror she discovers Dolly, her mum's cousin.

Other women arrive on the scene along with two men carrying a stretcher. Dolly is gently lifted onto the conveyance and transported to the office next to the main gate. By this time Gordon Hemmings has arrived along with Beryl Cooper, the latter having been informed that something has happened to her cousin. Susan, rummaging in her bag finds a bandage and dresses Dolly's head wound, then inspects her for any additional injuries. Dolly remains unconscious. There is little she can do but convey her findings to the doctor who has arrived with the ambulance, and comfort her mother.

'Is she going to survive, Susan?' Beryl asks, with a trembling voice.

'I don't know mum.'

'I think you had better go with her in the ambulance, Susan. The doctor can explain to you what the injuries are – you'll understand what he has to say better than me.'

'What are you going to do?'

‘I’ll go and pick up Charlie. He’ll want to know what has happened to his mum. And then I’ll bring him to the hospital.’

Mr Woods informs Gordon Hemmings that the small fires have been extinguished and that the cotton bundles have been soaked with water. Fortunately for everyone there are no fires in close proximity to the gunpowder and no more injuries.

Gordon Hemmings addresses Mr Woods. ‘Thanks for what you’ve done. I’ll leave you to sort the remainder out. I need to check up on Mrs Smith.’ He departs and catches up with Beryl.

‘I heard you talking to Susan and saying you are going to pick up Mrs Smith’s son.’

‘Yes.’

‘How are you getting there?’

‘I’ll have to walk to the school.’

‘That will take ages. Come with me, we’ll go in my car.’

It is not a great distance to the local ten-bed cottage hospital in Stone Street, but it is a busy time of the day. The ambulance driver has difficulty negotiating the oncoming trucks and cars from Chatham through Tanners Street before finally arriving at the hospital. Dolly is given priority treatment and the doctor administers morphine, while a nurse re-applies the dressing first put on by Susan. Dolly is still in a comatose state.

Susan insists on staying at the hospital. Not only does she wish to monitor Dolly's progress but she needs to be there when Beryl arrives with Dolly's son, Charlie. It is two hours later when the doctor returns to the hospital waiting room. He announces to the worried relatives and friends that they must expect the worse. The wound to her head, he says, is deeper and more serious than first anticipated, and if necessary she may have to be transferred to the hospital in Canterbury.

On seeing his mother Charlie becomes distraught, he sobs uncontrollably and is in great need of Beryl and Susan's assistance. It takes some considerable time to calm him down.

Back at the factory representatives from the Army and Munitions Board have arrived, along with the military Chief of Eastern Command. They are satisfied that no structural damage has incurred and that the remaining members of staff are safe: production will continue unimpeded. It is at this time that Gordon Hemmings gets a message from the hospital and sadly has to announce to the workers that Dolly Smith has died from the wound received.

On hearing the sad news many workers comfort each other with an embrace; others stand and cry whilst some remain standing in a state of shock. For someone to incur injury through an accident at work is one thing, but this was something quite out of the ordinary: this came as a complete shock. Amid the sobbing some curse the Hun with words of hatred: words of sorrow and venomous distain are expressed in equal measure. Dolly was a most popular and well-loved colleague. The manager is aware that Dolly's husband is in the Army and is stationed abroad. The question on his mind now is – who is going to notify him? He doesn't think Beryl or Susan would relish the idea, and so approaches the Chief of Eastern Command and asks his advice. The General promises to furnish him with her husband's name, rank and address, and that of his C.O. He thinks it best if Gordon informs the 'poor man', via his commanding officer, by letter. This Gordon promises to do.

Charlie is re-located to Beryl's house; she cannot possibly leave the boy alone. Susan moves into the bigger room with her mother and Charlie takes over Susan's bedroom. Not the best arrangement, but when Susan is on night shifts she stays at the hospital, so it is not as big an imposition as it otherwise might be.

Fourteen year old Charlie is due to leave school at the end of the term and Gordon Hemmings promises to secure him a job at the gunpowder works. Thus Beryl can keep an eye on him, and at least he will have a job.

In the interim, and understandably, Charlie withdraws into himself, preferring to internalise his hurt. Susan has had the opportunity to talk or rather listen to quite a few young soldiers, and so makes little attempt to question Charlie as to how he feels; young soldiers usually come to terms with their grief of losing close mates in their own time, so she employs this strategy with Charlie. If he has to communicate it is to her that he turns, whether this is because he is nearer her age or because of her nurse's uniform, no one is sure or asks.

Susan now has the very delicate and difficult task of writing to Harry and telling him about the tragic incident and its fatal outcome. She wonders if her letter will arrive before George has been delivered of Gordon Hemmings' letter via the commanding officer. Harry is advised, no matter how painful it is to him, not to say anything before George himself has been officially notified.

CHAPTER TWENTY

George Smith has acquired a new pal, Arthur Goode, who a year earlier and prior to being conscripted, was an apprentice joiner in Margate. He is young and his fresh face is in contrast to George's whose features contain ingrained lines bought on by age, and the tiring exertion of three years of fighting. They are soon to get to know each other better as they have been designated as the two forward look-outs at the sap-head. The sap-head is a particularly dangerous place to be positioned, as every soldier knows the shallow trench stretches outwards from the Front Line into non-man's land, terminating in an observation post.

George and Arthur are busy digging the earthworks for the parados when work ceases as the enemy traverses its machine guns in their direction. Soon the cry 'Stretcher bearer!' is heard.

'I bet it's Sap 13 – that's where we're going,' George says, sitting down behind his shovel.

'What day is it?' asks Arthur.

'It's Friday, Friday the thirteenth. You know what that means don't yer?'

'Our lucky day; that's all we need!' remarks Arthur with heavy irony.

Captain East arrives and looks earnestly at the two privates. 'It's time to move to the sap-head lads. I need you to stay there as long as you can. We're short of men and none can be spared to remain in support. If you get into trouble send up a couple of Verey lights and hurry back to the front line. Sergeant Cooper and I will meet you at the entrance to the sap in a short while.' They gather, along with rifle and ammunition, a couple of Mills bombs, and their additional equipment: binoculars and compass; equipment they may need to identify enemy positions.

They arrive at the sap entrance and wait for the Captain and the Sergeant. On arrival Captain East gives the Verey light pistol to Arthur and Harry hands George a couple of letters. 'Here you are, but don't be reading your letters at the same time. Make sure one of you has his eyes peeled,' orders Harry.

'I'm afraid it's going to be a long night. I'll have you relieved as soon as possible but I doubt if it will be before morning. Sergeant Cooper has a bit of grub for you,' indicates the Captain pointing at the small parcel.

Harry hands over a bag and tells them to lead on. Arthur slots the package into his small pack. 'You'll find it ankle deep in mud so it will be difficult at first.'

The first part of the journey isn't too hard and to help progress the intermittent shelling has ceased. The second part is much more difficult. It is akin to walking through the thickest of gluey quicksand. Each step is an effort and the sound of suction as boots are pulled out of the quagmire pierces the night's temporary silence. Every noise a soldier makes at failing light is disconcerting. 'I bet they can bloody well hear us coming', bemoans George.

They eventually reach a hole where the support bay was a short while ago; it's now just another depression in the ground. 'How much further to go?' asks Captain East.

'About seventy five feet,' replies Sergeant Cooper.

'OK you two, you have ten minutes to reach the end of the sap. Unless you signal us before that we'll return to the front-line trench. Be careful. Good luck!' With that the Captain looks at his watch and the two forward observers move off with the Verey lights and mills bombs that they have collected on route, plus capes and their rifles. It's not very far to travel but in the gloom and through glutinous mud and on all fours, it takes longer than expected to reach the sap-end. The sight of the enemy's front line is becoming clearer as eyes become more accustomed to the dark and night vision improves.

The intrepid two arrive at their station and settle down in a semi-prone position. They talk in lowered tones. 'You know the two things I hated most before the war,' whispers Arthur: 'Digging the clay soil in the allotment with my dad, and going on our annual camping expedition with the scouts, when it always bloody rained. My dad insisted I did both; now sodding look at me!'

'Ever the optimist, it could be worse. We're as snug as a couple of bugs in a rug, save for the odd squatting rats.' George kicks out at two soaking wet vermin scurrying up the side of the muddy bank.

'So who made you join the Army?' enquires Arthur.

'The King, the Government, the wife and me bleedin' relatives … but not necessarily in that order.'

'Your wife ... don't she like you? Does she want a divorce?'

'No it's not that. She's got a job in an explosives factory, so she's doing her bit, and my cousin in-law, who, as yer know is our illustrious sergeant; but the main reason, believe it or not, came from me teenage son. He looked at me as if to say, 'Well dad, what are yer going to do for the war effort?'

'No pressure then!'

'I'll take the first stag,' says George, raising the binoculars. 'You see if there is enough light to read your letter and see what grub we've got. Hopefully someone will arrive with some rum-laced tea later.' With that George peers through a small gap in their defences and surveys the scene. The light from the full moon casts eerie shadows across the bleak landscape. There remains the odd stump of a tree here and there, and discarded sections of rolled barbed wire where the front line once was – thus indicating the minimal movement forward and backwards either side has made. It is a lighted moonscape of depression, both geographical and mental. An enemy flare is launched and George ducks down aware of the danger of enemy snipers; not wanting to lose his night vision he shields his eyes.

Arthur chuckles. 'What you laughing about?' whispers George.

'I just think it's very considerate of the Boche to switch the light on so you can read your letter.'

The temperature begins to drop rapidly and the front-line spotters wrap themselves more tightly in their groundsheets. Arthur determines to get a short nap while George takes charge of the Verey pistol. He checks his ammunition state and positions the mills bombs nearby ready for throwing, if required. George opens his wallet, and as he does every evening, and kisses the photo of his wife and boy. Adjusting his position, he scans more closely the enemy lines which are uncomfortably near, only about three hundred or so yards away. His other concern is to keep awake. He decides to leave the sleeping Arthur for the present; he'll wake him later on when he feels it's time to eat.

Captain Peter East and Sergeant Harry Cooper have waited the agreed ten minutes. There has been no call from Privates Smith and Goode, so they make their way back to their main front-line trench.

‘I’ll get the platoon commander to do a check on the lads later, you come with me Sergeant. I think we deserve a little snifter.’

‘That’s an enlightened decision, if I may say so sir,’ says Harry Cooper with a grin.

They duck down into the entombed office with its supports of wood and walls of mud. Captain East grasps the half-full bottle of Scotch and pours out two generous amounts into the tin mugs.

‘Have you got the mail, Harry?

‘Yes, here it is.

I see I’ve got a letter from your home town, Faversham.’ Captain Peter East tears open the envelope. ‘It’s from the gunpowder factory.’ He reads the letter written by Gordon Hemmings, the general manager. There is a pause before the Captain exclaims, ‘Oh my God! Private Smith is part of your family, isn’t he?’

‘Yes, his wife is my wife’s cousin. So what’s the problem, sir?’

‘Have you got a letter from home?’

‘Yes.’

‘Read it, I suspect it will tell you what I’ve just read.’

Harry is concerned by his company commander’s startled reaction and hurriedly rips open his envelope. He quickly scans the letter from Susan and echoes his captain’s words. ‘Oh! My God! Jesus Christ! Poor Dolly … I hope Beryl has seen to their boy Charlie.’

The commander asks, ‘do you think Smith has read his letter yet?’

‘I don’t know, but we can’t leave him out there at the end of the sap. Christ knows what state he’ll be in when he does.’

‘I’ll send somebody out to get him.’

‘No sir, I’ll go, this is family business’, says Harry sharply.

Arthur wakes with a start at the sap-head and asks George what time it is. ‘Time we swopped positions. Time I read my letter from home.’

Apart from the odd sound of the zip of a rifle bullet in the distance the night is quiet. The enemy is lighting up the sky with more Verey lights. The still, frosty and shivering silent air is suddenly rent asunder when George emits an anguished primeval howl. ‘For Christ’s sake George what’s up?’ asks a concerned Arthur. George’s appears doubled-up as in pain. His hands are shaking; he clasps his head and begins to wail uncontrollably.

‘The bastards, the bastards,’ he screams, ‘they’ve bloody killed her, they’ve killed me wife.’

Arthur attempts to calm him down while trying to find out more about what has so disturbed him.

George’s shouts, curses and groans are heard by Harry Cooper who is desperately trying to get through the glutinous mud along the sap in order to extricate George from his position. He also needs to silence him although the enemy must have heard everything, and so there is no point in the boys remaining in that forward post.

It begins to rain heavily which masks the moon’s light to a great extent. Thank God for that thinks Harry. It’ll make it more difficult for a German sniper to take aim. By the time Harry arrives George is shaking and sobbing uncontrollably.

Arthur attempts to explain what has happened. Harry ignores him and grabs George. Holding his rifle in one hand, attempts to drag him out of the sap-head. ‘Give me a hand, Goode and don’t ask questions.’ They grip George’s webbing straps and physically haul him back towards their trench. This, thankfully, coincides with a British barrage which keeps the enemies heads down. It takes some time to reach safety, by which time they are joined by the company sergeant-major. George is yanked unceremoniously down onto the duckboards, and out of the line of fire. They run him back along the trench and away from the sap entrance. The rain and short barrage has stopped and it is hoped that things, including Private George Smith’s hysterical actions, will calm down.

While Arthur and Sergeant Cooper are regaining their breath Captain East tells George Smith that they will try to get him back to Blighty A.S.A.P. George is deaf to all this. He stands there full of enraged grief, cursing loudly he shouts ‘Fucking bastards, fucking bastards, you bloody wait.’ He jumps to his feet, makes a grab for his rifle which is lying against the front wall of the trench; before anyone could re-act George yells again, ‘I’ll get you, you murdering bastards!’ With that he slides back the bolt and forces a round into the breach. The Sergeant-major makes to restrain him but George is too quick, and he jumps up onto the fire step, his head above the parapet. There is the sound of a rifle being fired. George buckles at the knees. His helmet tumbles forward. His torso collapses to the ground.

The men are stunned. They stand in awestruck silence. Captain East calls for stretcher bearers, even though they know it's pointless.

Sergeant Harry Cooper follows the stretcher down the winding wooden, sandbag-lined causeway. There is nothing he can do but detach George's identity discs and hand them in, take the letter from his pocket – along with the photograph – and later ensure they are sent home for his son. Then return to the front-line trench.

Young Arthur has been given a mug of tea with a slug of rum and returns to be with his pals.

Captain East and the sergeant-major are waiting for Harry with a mug of tea in the commander's dug-out. 'Here you are Harry. Let's put something a bit stronger in that,' he says emptying the last tot of whisky into Harry's mug.

'Are you OK?' enquires the Captain.

'Yeah, I'll cope,' replies Harry shaking.

'Tell me sergeant, who do I write to? Now he's got no wife. Are his parents still alive?'

‘No. Someone will have to write to his son.’

‘How old is his son?’ asks Captain East.

‘Fourteen.’

‘You’ll have to give me some advice,’ says Captain East.

‘Yes … you better send it to my home address,’ says Harry Cooper. ‘I expect he will be staying at my house. There’s nowhere else for the poor little beggar to go. I’ve got to write to my wife.’

CHAPTER TWENTY-ONE

The news is received with profound sadness at the factory. Beryl and Susan do their best to comfort young Charlie. He cannot be consoled. He is encouraged to go to work at the factory; there is nothing else for him to do. The place where his mother worked evokes painful memories. He finds it hard to release his emotions and cry; he becomes withdrawn, retreating into an un-penetrative emotional shell, shutting himself in his room – only communicating in monosyllables.

‘Did you get a letter this morning?’ asks Beryl seeing the pleasing grin on her daughter’s face.

‘Yes. Is Charlie still in bed?’

‘Yes, he won’t be down for a while. He seems to be making himself at home in your room. When your father comes home we will have to move house. You and I can’t keep sharing a room and you can’t share with Charlie – he’s too old for that.’

‘I can’t wait to read James’ letters but I hate to read the news from James when Charlie’s around.’ Susan opens the letter and gives a little squeal of delight. ‘He says he’s been promoted. That means he’s got another pip, he’s now a fully-fledged Lieutenant. The rest is the usual guarded messages and words of affection.’ She kisses the letter and puts it in the pocket of her uniform to be read later, many times.

‘I do miss him, mum. But there is something I have to tell you,’ she says with a concerned look on her face.

‘Well, go ahead, don’t be bashful. Although I think I know what it might be about. It’ll be about us not sharing a bedroom. Am I right?’ This is more a statement than a question from Beryl.

‘I don’t know how you do it, mum. Are you a ruddy clairvoyant?’

'No dear, I'm just your mother. Don't forget I've known you longer than anyone else. So, are you going to tell me, or do I have to make an educated guess?'

'I did mention to you some time ago that they're looking for temporary assistants at the hospital in France. And … well … I was thinking of volunteering.'

'It can't be to get a room of your own; you'll have to share with others I expect. I'm sure it isn't just for philanthropic reasons? Or is this in the hope of possibly seeing your beloved, that newly promoted and good looking young lieutenant?'

'You know the real reason … Mum, you can be so irritatingly smug at times. You don't mind do you?'

'Of course I mind. I'd rather my only child didn't put herself in danger. But I understand: you want to see the man you love. If things had been different and we were not at war, I expect I'd be planning to be a grandmother,' says Beryl, embracing her daughter.

'Why are you hugging each other like that?' inquires Charlie in an unusually longer sentence, as he enters the kitchen.

Then to Charlie's delight Susan embraces him. They have become quite close and as she is the nearest to him in age he feels that they have more in common with each other, besides she has given up her room for him. Although he doesn't open up conversationally, he knows that when he's depressed Susan will come and sit by him; she'll not always speak but her presence acts as a comfort.

'Well I'm going to be away for a bit. I'm off to work in a hospital in France. Oh, and there is no need to look so glum Charlie, it'll only be for a short time.'

Beryl looks at her daughter, and attempts to give her some advice. 'There's no guarantee that you will be able to see him. You know that, don't you? I wouldn't expect the matron or the commanding officer to be helpful. They'll expect you to work night and day, so I doubt if there will be any time for socialising or, in your case, canoodling.'

'I don't care, mum. I'll be happy to see him just once. You never know it might be the one and only … the last time', Susan begins to cry.

'Now that's enough of that my girl. Pull yourself together and let me know when you're going. Charlie and I will travel to Folkestone on the train and see you off. It'll be exciting, won't it Charlie?' Charlie merely nods while trying to affect a smile.

This is the third ‘farewell’ for Beryl, and in one way the hardest. She expected her husband to go eventually. By saying ‘goodbye’ to Susan, albeit hopefully, only temporarily, means she is losing her confidante. Susan, now a woman, and the only other adult at home has become her mother’s best friend; besides which, she shares the burden of looking after Charlie.

The death of Dolly, and then George so quickly plays continuously on Beryl’s mind; having to worry about Harry is bad enough, and now knowing her daughter will be in danger reduces her to tears. She does her very best to hid her fears from Susan. Charlie is also feeling added strain, on one occasion he catches Beryl lamenting the forthcoming departure of Susan. Without restraint he embraces Beryl, shares her grief and they console each other - tearfully.

It is a grey overcast sky the morning that Beryl and Charlie wave goodbye to Susan at Westgate-on-Sea station. Beryl wants to take the day off and travel to Folkestone. Susan insists that she shouldn’t. Standing on the quayside would be too painful, they would all be blubbering in public and that wouldn’t do. Better to do the crying at home. Her mother, as expected, can’t stop herself weeping and Charlie does his best to fight back the tears; he has become more than fond of Susan, he secretly has a crush on her.

Whilst on the boat Susan ponders the departure from England, her eyes are brimming with tears. This emotion is eventually eclipsed by the need to see James. Passengers disembark in army fashion; senior officers first, junior officers and nurses next and then the remaining other ranks. The ship blows its mournful horn. The Channel crossing passes without incident; the black inky waters spread feelings of gloom for those returning; Susan cannot openly admit to feelings tinged with subdued excitement.

It doesn't take long on the slow jangling train from Boulogne to Etaples. The eighteen mile journey is over in less than an hour; approaching from the south the passengers get some idea of the size of the encampment. A heavy downpour had just ceased. The roadway was liquid with mud. Susan is making mental notes of the various camps within the larger compound. On the left is the cemetery and mortuary. On the right is a Segregation Camp – for whom she wonders. And opposite are the infamous sand dunes with tufts of spikey grass that dad had told her about. She can see squads of soldiers running up and down along the hillocks with heavy packs on their backs, carrying rifles with clipped on fixed-bayonets. They look exhausted. There are other unidentifiable buildings. To the left of the station is a large chateau, presumably this is where the headquarter staff live and work. On showing her pass to a transport officer she is directed down the Rue de Camiers and along the seafront to the

Women's Hostel on the other side of the rail tracks, next to a large quarry.

A smallish woman in a nurse's cape comes forward to meet Susan. 'Hello, you've got to be Susan Cooper. How are you, my dear?' pronounced 'm'dear' by Nurse Doris Beech. She must, judging by the burr sound of her voice, come from somewhere in the West Country thinks Susan. The elongated vowels make her sound welcoming and it's comforting. It soon becomes apparent that she usually completes each communication with the phrase m'dear no matter who she is talking to. The doctors find it quite amusing and all the patients referred to her as Nurse M'dear. Even the hospital's senior nursing personnel don't mind being spoken to in this fashion. It is doubly amusing to hear her say, 'Yes, sir, m'dear.' However, she does manage to refrain from addressing matron in this fashion. She is a Red Cross nurse, and therefore not military; if she was in the Army Medical Corps things may be different.

They finish their coffee in the YMCA centre and head back along the Rue de Camiers towards the station; but instead of turning right they veer left past the Machine Gun School and the Chateau, then head north past a Canadian Hospital to No. 26 General Hospital. 'Number 26, goodness me,' says Susan. 'How many hospitals are there?'

‘Well, let me see,’ muses Doris. ‘No. 46 is the Isolation Hospital and No. 51 is the Allied Forces hospital. There are now separate hospitals for the Americans and a General Hospital for officers, and one run by St John Ambulance in addition to all the ones used by British, Australian and other Empire Forces. I don’t know the exact number.’

‘The mind boggles!’

‘That’s not all. There are also about ten training camps and a detention camp or two. The detention camp is quite full at the moment due to a recent mutiny. They say it was provoked by the Red Caps, that’s the military police. Anyway, things have quietened down now, but there’s still a bit of tension among the soldiers. Well, here we are. I’ve been told to take you to Matron’s office, m’dear. She insists on vetting all new-comers herself.’

‘She sounds like a bit of a dragon.’

‘You got it in one, m’dear. Still, only to be expected, after all she is Welsh.’ says Doris laughing.

The hospital comprises row upon row of wooden huts. They are all much larger than the local hospital accommodation at home where she worked. Susan knocks on the door of the administration centre and is ushered into a large ante-room, the walls of which are stacked with filing cabinets. Two

doors lead off at the far end, one of which is marked Matron. An orderly takes her name and reports to the adjoining office. 'Right, wheel her in, Corporal,' the responding voice calls.
It is with feelings of trepidation that Susan finds herself standing in front of the 'dragon's' desk. In the swivel chair sits a woman in her fifties or sixties, grey haired, with tight lips and acquisitive features. 'Welcome to Etaples, Cooper. I must say that I am pleased to see that you are not a total beginner. We really do not have time to train nurses here. The size of this hospital, not to mention the whole encampment, will come as a bit of a shock at first, but you'll soon get used to it.' She looks at Susan with penetrating eyes that strip any confidence from the new arrival. After a short awkward pause she continues. 'I expect only three things from my staff. First, cleanliness – there are over 20,000 patients under treatment in these hospitals, and a further 50,000 soldiers in training at any one time. Disease can spread like wildfire, so hygiene is of paramount importance. Secondly, discipline – I do not tolerate lateness, laxity of any sort or fraternisation. You will be seen as an 'angel of mercy' to these boys and some of them will inevitably think that they have fallen in love with you – you cannot allow yourself to reciprocate. Remember they have family at home, and you have many other patients to deal with. And thirdly, dedication: we are here for a specific purpose, to serve the patients and the country, any questions?'

'Er, no Matron.'

‘Good, you are dismissed.’

Susan makes her way across the road to her billet, which is a long dormitory in another wooden hut. Two rows of ten beds line the walls either side of a narrow strip down the centre. Each nurse has a locker by the head of her bed. In the middle of the billet is a cast iron stove. The positioning of a person’s bed is therefore critical. The newer arrivals occupy the beds furthest from the stove, not the best position to be in during the cold winter months. At the end of the hut is a separate room for a staff nurse. The ablutions are located in an adjoining hut. Anyone complaining is reminded that all the soldiers in training are housed in tents.

Susan is reminded of the VAD quarters at home, which was a step-down from the nurses’ accommodation. Although now a nurse she was at the bottom of this pile.

Doris is her chaperone for the day, after which she will be on her own. ‘Well, what do you think? It takes some adjusting. Living in a room full of girls is not what some of us are used to, m’dear. Many of the Voluntary Aid Detachment girls and some of the nurses who went to boarding schools have no trouble adjusting: this is how they were bought up. You didn’t go to a posh school, m’dear – did you?’

‘Certainly not,’ replies Susan.

It doesn't take long to fill the small locker with her minimum belongings. Doris helps her make up the bed and they sit there while 'm'dear' chats on. Other soon to be familiar sounds can be heard. The Machine Gun School is in full use and the rat-a-tat-tat of the guns on the range can be heard, with intermittent yelling of orders from the instructors on the sand dunes. 'Don't worry m'dear, you'll get used to it. Now it's time for us to do the rounds and for you to meet the ward sister. No need for you to look so concerned m'dear.'

It is a short walk across the road to the hospital. 'Sister Bridget, here is our newest recruit', announces Doris. Sister Bridget appears the antithesis of Matron. She is in her thirties, with red hair, high cheek bones and a generous figure. Facially she could be a model, thinks Susan. 'I expect you are used to filling just one small ward at a time in England. In contrast, last night for example, we admitted 110 soldiers between 1 and 4 am. And that was just the first of three convoys; half of them medical, the other half surgical. If you have any initial problems talk to Nurse Beech here, if she can't help, come to me. Have you any questions?'

For the second time that day Susan felt a bit overawed and could think of nothing to say, so she merely shook her head.
'No. Good. You will be assigned to a medical ward for the time being. You will be doing much the same work as in England, only there will be a lot more patients to deal with. Later you may be re-located to a surgical ward.'

Prior to admittance the patients at home had received the initial treatment and so their wounds were not so raw. Here the burns victims were terrifying at first. Susan had never heard men scream so loud. On occasions her assistance is confined to holding the soldier's hand while the doctor or the sister changes the blood-soaked adhesive dressings. The squeeze by a man's hand in such circumstances can be painful, but that is a price worth paying when she witnesses the result of treatment. The soldiers' gratitude can be overwhelming. Susan is reminded of what Sister Bridget and Matron said to her, 'You are an angel of mercy, not of love.'

One night she witnesses Sister Bridget's compassion. She is comforting a young soldier who is too young to be in the Army; he is only seventeen and should still be at home. As a result of his mortal wounds he is placed in a screened-off bed at the end of the ward. In the early hours of the morning the sound of sobbing can be heard. Susan peers around the screen to see the boy in the arms of Sister Bridget. Between wails of tears he is calling for his mother. Sister, her cheeks moist, clasps him to her bosom and rocks him gently back and forth. Even the most experienced and battle-hardened nurse cannot be immune to suffering, particularly when it affects the young. He dies two hours later.

Susan is reminded of fourteen year old Charlie and wonders how he is coping; and how her mother is managing to bring up young Charlie.

CHAPTER TWENTY-TWO

'That was a long walk Charlie. Where have you been?' asks Beryl.

'Out' comes the abrupt reply.

It is difficult to talk to youths, at the best of times, thinks Beryl, and therefore decides not to pursue this line of enquiry; his mode of retort suggests that he's never likely to get over the death of both his parents, particularly as they died in tragic circumstances, and in quick succession. But after a year Beryl thinks he might begin to cope a little better. She cannot berate him for his seemingly surly, dismissive and rude manner; that, she believes, would be too cruel. The boy is a conscientious worker, the men at the factory say so, adding that he carries out his tasks in a state of almost 'manic concentration'. It is, of course, his way of coping, venting his anger at the Hun. Beryl is of a mind that Charlie wants to get closer to the enemy.

On their occasional walk to the seafront, although not along the beach – this is still out of bounds and anyone penetrating the rolls of barbed wire court a penal punishment – Beryl attempts to converse with Charlie. While looking left across the water to Maplin Sands and right across the Channel, Beryl tries to interest the boy in the wildlife, but he only has eyes for the military. The ships and aircraft proceeding to

London from the continent are of consummate interest. One evening they watch a squad of soldiers marching along the esplanade, bayonets glistening in the evening sun. She notices Charlie standing upright as they approach. He sticks his chest out as they come level to where he is standing; he turns, and marches onward in time with them for several yards.

'I suppose it is a natural reaction,' says Beryl to her friend Jean.

'But he's not little – well he is little – but he's not a *very* young boy anymore, is he?' replies her friend.

'No, he isn't.'

'How old is he?'

'He's fourteen and a bit. He's been out of school for nearly a year.'

'Well' comments Jean in a consoling voice, 'he's got another couple of years or so to go before he can legally don uniform.'

'Yes, I suppose you're right. It's just there's a few over there who are under age. I got a letter this morning from our Susan who told me about a seventeen year old who died in the arms of one of the nurses. It's a heart-rending tale. It had me in tears, I don't mind telling you. I don't want Charlie to end up like that. I wish our Susan was back here. She could talk to him; she's the only one he listens to.'

'You'll have to keep an eye on him Beryl – see that he doesn't sneak off.'

Beryl tries to ensure that her shifts coincide with Charlie's. It's not that she distrusts him, totally; rather it is her protective mothering instinct and sense of duty to her late cousin that determines her actions. This means that most of the time they arrive and leave home and factory together. When at home, during the lighter evenings, he disappears for hours on end fishing, an interest he acquired from his dad. There is nothing wrong with that, but he also takes himself off on long isolated walks. Where he goes, Beryl is not always certain. Friends tell of seeing him on the cliff tops watching the naval activity out at sea and any military goings-on along the coast nearby. Nothing strange in that either: he is a boy and it is quite natural that he should be interested in manly things; perhaps more so these days as there is a war on. Nevertheless, Beryl feels a twinge of unease.

On Friday night Beryl emerges from the brick bunker where she works and makes her way to the factory gates to wait for Charlie. On arrival at the exit she hears the steady beat of drums and the accompanying sound of bugles. The musical cacophony emanates from the centre of Faversham.

A Royal Artillery Battery is visiting the town. The blurb in the local press state that it is for the purposes of saying 'thank you' to the munitioneers, a public way of acknowledging the important work they are doing. Parked under the stilted Guildhall building in the centre of town is a gun carriage and horses. Children are allowed to clamber over the limber of the gun-carriage and to pat the steeds. A band is arranged in the middle of the square and a crowd of people, now being swelled by additional workers from the factories, listen appreciatively to the music.

Charlie has purposely arrived before Beryl. He scans the scene and looks around for someone who he thinks can further his cause.

Charlie draws himself up to his full height, pulls his cap down to try and hide a part of his young face and puts on, what he considers a serious and mature expression before approaching a soldier. Charlie halts before the soldier and stands firmly to attention before stating his business. 'Excuse me sir, I want to talk to the recruiting person. I want to join the Army.'

'Do yer now, what's yer name son?'

'Charlie.'

'Charlie what … Chaplin?'

'No. Charlie Smith.'

'Ah! A little Smudger.'

'No. Smith.'

'In the Army Charlie boy, 'Smiff', says the soldier, who is obviously a cockney from the East End of London, 'Smith is known as Smudger. Now then, Mr Smudger Smiff, how tall is yer?'

'I'm five feet six,' Sergeant.'

'Well done! You got my rank right, but I gotta say you aren't as tall as you say, Smudger. I'm five foot seven and you just about come up to my shoulder.' In truth, Charlie is the product of below average sized parents; his father who was a little taller than his mother, at just five feet three, plus a couple more inches when wearing his boots. Charlie has marginally outgrown the height attained by his mother, although he is still below the requisite height to join the Army.

‘I’m fit you know. I work at the factory – I’m lifting 50 pound shells every day.’ This is not a lie – Charlie has become immensely strong for his size. It is at this point that Beryl, now out of breath, reaches Charlie and the Sergeant. Before she can utter a word the Sergeant raises his hand and bids her stop. Beryl is crestfallen. Has the stupid boy enlisted? The Sergeant winks knowingly at Beryl; then holds out his hand palm down about three inches above Charlie’s head. ‘Now jump,’ he commands, and ‘see if you can reach me hand with yer head.’

‘Is this a physical test?’ inquires Charlie.

‘Yeah … sort of.’

Charlie jumps and heads the outstretched palm.

‘Very good Smudger, you’ve obviously also got strong legs, but the problem is you didn’t stay there. If you could reach me hand by not jumping, then you would be tall enough to join the Army.’

Charlie is demoralised. He has no answer. ‘Now look Charlie-boy, yer didn’t fail. It’s just that yer need to come back later when yer taller. Take off yer hat.’ His brown hair drops forward and covers one eye. The Sergeant glances at Beryl who at this point is smiling, and fixes Charlie with a beady military eye. ‘How old is he misses?’

Beryl could have said fourteen but for Charlie's sake she replies, 'almost fifteen.'

'Smudger' the Sergeant says laying a fatherly hand on his shoulder. 'I don't know what made yer want to enlist early but I can guess. We're here today to thank people like you for the great job you're doing – we're proud of yer – so when you grow a bit more come back and join my regiment; you're a brave boy and soon enough, you'll be a man.' Beryl puts a hand on Charlie's arm before leading him away and mouthing a 'thank you' to the Sergeant.

Charlie, head down, leaves the scene with aunty Beryl, as he now calls her. But he purposely walks a yard distant from her as he doesn't want anyone to think he is being led away by an older female member of the family. He is desperately trying to shake off the shackles of adolescence and appear a man. Beryl is sensitive to his thoughts and feelings and says nothing.

That night she writes to Susan describing the events of the day, asking her to write a letter especially for Charlie and to send it directly to him.

Two weeks later Charlie receives the missive from Susan. In the letter she explains how she misses home, her mum and him. Her letter is frank and mature; the incident with the under-age boy and the Sister in the hospital is recounted. She adds that in the not-too-distant future when, hopefully, she has met James, she will be returning home. Her words act as a step in the direction of his development – some might say emotional convalescence – as he feels that he is, at last, being understood and treated as a mature person. He still appears distant when communicating with Beryl, but at least he now takes time to discuss, albeit in a perfunctory manner, the contents of the letter.

CHAPTER TWENTY-THREE

Susan is delighted to get a response to the letter she sent to Charlie. It isn't a long reply. He writes in a staccato fashion rather than complete sentences but that is how he speaks, so it is to be expected. As happy as Susan is to receive news from Charlie and her mother, there are two other people she really wants to hear from.

Her father, now that he is the platoon sergeant, says he has even less time to write. 'I expect', she comments to nurse Doris, 'now that he has greater responsibility he is probably pre-occupied, looking after his men even when they're not fighting.'

'That's no real excuse. I expect he has written but you know what the mail system is like. His letter is probably sitting in the bottom of a sack in the post-master's orderly room. Have you checked your pigeon hole in the office lately, m'dear?'

'Let's go and check it now. In truth I'm finding it difficult to know what to write about. I think my letters must be sounding like a medical report. What I would like to do is get out of camp and explore the town of Etaples.'

'Are you sure about that? There is nothing interesting or edifying in Etaples, m'dear.'

'Maybe not, but I still want to see it,' retorts Susan. Her reply sounds more like an order than a request. Doris, although a little surprised by her companion's sharpish manner, agrees to go with her to Etaples the next day – their half-day off.

On arrival at the outer limits of the camp Susan and Doris have to step aside as a company of troops come 'tramp, tramp' down the road heading for the notorious training areas known as the 'Bull Ring'. Judging by the soldiers' sweat-stained faces they are completing a route march.

The pair stroll up the Rue de la Gare towards the station. The streets of Etaples are very narrow; in places buildings are no more than three yards apart. Worse still they are filthy with open drains: the stench is something awful. The village is caught in a mediaeval time-warp. The women look tired, worn out and dirty. In the centre of the village is the ubiquitous square with a stone building where Napoleon once stayed. It is now a wine store. A market is held in the square twice a week and, Doris tells Susan, it is where pigeons and rabbits are killed as and when required. 'I don't think I'd like to do my shopping there, no matter how fresh the food is supposed to be,' comments Susan.

The two nurses continue their walk, but now with handkerchiefs covering their faces; the stench in places is almost suffocating. Passing one particular street Susan spots several soldiers waiting by a doorway. 'I wonder what they are waiting for?' enquires Susan.

'What do you think, m'dear Susan … you can't be that green!'

'Why do they do it, Doris?'

'Because, m'dear, they're men with an instinctive urge which, presumably, they can't control. Before you go on to condemn them, remember most of them are young and have never been with a woman. And they believe the chances are they'll probably be dead before they get the opportunity.'

'Oh!'

'Now let's go back to camp and wash before visiting the YMCA canteen for a cup of tea. When we get there you can tell me the real reason why you wanted to visit the Etaples town centre.'

'What do you mean?' asks Susan.

'You know very well what I mean, m'dear'.

The YMCA canteen occupies a part of a large hut which can seat up to 400 people when there is a show on. Its main function is supposed to be for religious services, but the pantomimes, revues and sing-songs are more popular. During the daytime on a weekday it doubles as a canteen. An upright piano stands against the wall in the far corner next to the stage. Anyone with the ability to play is encouraged to do so, and it is often in use. There seems to be an endless supply of pub pianists so there is never a shortage of accompaniment during the organised sing-songs. However, there is one soldier who the two nurses believe was a professional musician before he was conscripted into the Army. During his spare time when convalescing he entertains himself and others with classical pieces. Today he is playing Beethoven's *Moonlight Sonata.* Some people think that listening to music composed by a German is somehow unpatriotic, but most are of the opinion that great music transcends international boundaries. Susan and Doris enjoy the man's playing, listen in silence, and along with others clap his efforts when he has completed the piece. The pianist turns and nods in acknowledgement to the scattered audience.

‘So who’s the letter from today, m’dear?’ enquires Doris.

‘It’s from my dad. He’s obviously non-committal about what they’re doing or where they are – the censor sees to that, look at the crossings-out. It worries me. I think the less he says, the more fighting he must be doing. He says the thing he looks forward to most is my wedding and that the sooner that takes place the better. He hopes to be home for some leave before long.’ With a dispiriting shrug Susan concludes ‘the chances of him and James getting leave at the same time may never happen, so he says we’re to go ahead with the wedding whether he’s there or not. Oh, Doris, I want my dad there. It wouldn’t be the same without him.’

Doris looks hard and enquiringly at Susan, pauses and says, ‘I do believe that what you have just told me is not totally unconnected to our trip to Etaples. Am I correct in this assumption, m’dear?’

‘What gives you that impression?’

‘The fact that when we were walking around town you asked about places to stay, also that you are engaged, and that your fiancée is over here and in uniform. It is obvious that you can’t wait to be married … in fact you have talked about nothing else!’

‘Oh, is it that obvious?’

'Yes, m'dear … and it's right that it should be. So I suppose we'll have to find somewhere for you both to stay. How long has he got, and when is he coming?'

'In a week's time and it's just for thirty-six hours.'

'In that case, tomorrow we will visit Le Trèport.'

Doris had confided in Sister Bridget and told her of their intention to visit the nearby town of Le Trèport; she knows that sister is more lenient when it comes to mixing with officers. Matron does not like the idea of fraternization with anyone outside the medical services. She adheres to the military dictate that husbands and wives, indeed any relative of the opposite sex, should not serve within close proximity of each other. Some mandarins believe that such liaisons would make other men jealous. Besides, they opine that a man's concentration – hence his efficiency – may be impeded by having a loved one in the vicinity. Although Susan is not married, matron is likely to say that the latter would apply to fiancées – perhaps even more so, given the likely age and emotional involvement of such a couple.

Prior to the nurses' departure, the following afternoon Sister Bridget calls them into her office and reminds them of matron's rules. Susan looks a little downcast. 'You mean I can't even hold his hand.'

‘Preferably not in public Nurse Cooper, what you do in private is entirely up to you,’ she adds with a knowing smile. She then slides a card across the table on which is written an address. Pointing to the card she adds smilingly, ‘take that, you might find it useful. Do take care of her Nurse Beech – she’s likely to get over excited. We have a truck with supplies going to the Hotel Trianon, the General Hospital in Le Trèport, it leaves tomorrow afternoon – I suggest you be at the guard room by the camp entrance at 1400 hours.’

Doris detects Susan’s excitement the moment they vacate Sister’s office. ‘She is an absolute brick,’ exclaims Susan.

‘Yes, but remember what she said. If Matron finds out what you’re planning she’ll be looking to send you straight home, m’dear.’

‘She wouldn’t do that.’

‘Wouldn’t she? I think she might!’

The short drive to Le Trèport presents a different picture, the fields of poppies and wild flowers being a pleasant alternative to the slum-like grime of Etaples and the boring lines of tents and huts of the camp. Le Trèport, on the other side of the Canche River, is a small fishing port and seaside town located at the foot of high, white cliffs where the Bresle River joins the English Channel, not unlike the coastal resorts at home in north-east Kent. The truck is halted by a sentry on the bridge before being allowed to continue. 'Why have they stopped us?' inquires Susan. 'Because Le Trèport is officer territory and they try to keep the other ranks out, although you can walk across at low tide. This was where a soldier was shot by a military policeman and a mutiny started, but enough of that; we have more pleasant things to do – have we not?'

The Hotel Trianon is a huge grandiose looking building with an ornate balustrade and turrets, the sort of expensive venue that neither Susan nor Doris could afford to stay when on vacation. An imposing staircase swept up to the front doors. It has been converted to a hospital; its vast surrounding grounds are covered in white tents and marquees of varying shapes and sizes.

The nurses thank the driver and decide to amble along the verdant cliff top overlooking the sea. A quarter of a mile further on they come to a small hillock and sit down.

'How come you know this town?' asks Susan.

'It's a long story,' says Doris, her mouth tightens indicating a slight grimace.

'Do tell', asks Susan, she is concerned by the reaction to her question, but also intrigued to know more. 'Come on' she continues, 'you've heard my darkest secrets now I want to know yours. I have a feeling our experiences are not totally unconnected. Am I right in this assumption?'

'As far as you have gone, yes you are m'dear. Yes, I had a secret assignation with a young soldier here in Le Trèport. He was a Captain in the Engineers. He was so handsome, so charming. We walked along this very route.'

'Where did you meet him, Doris?'

'In the hospital, he was one of my patients. I should have listened to what Matron had to say about fraternization but I didn't. I suppose I was swept off my feet. Captain Herbert Good MC he'd say; he'd always salute before sweeping me into his arms. I'd have done anything for him. I adored him. When he was convalescing we'd go out for walks, later we stayed at a little hotel along the seafront.'

'Sounds wonderful,' says Susan.

'It was. I'd never been so happy. Captain Good was very, very good … but then I lost him.'

'Oh, I'm so sorry to hear that. When was he killed?'

'He wasn't. It was worse than that.'

‘What can be worse than being killed? He couldn’t have been that badly injured or you wouldn’t have been able to walk out with him, would you?’

‘He was sent back to England’.

‘And …’

‘To be with his wife, and kids!’

‘Oh!’

‘At least you won’t have to face that problem Susan, m’dear.’

They continue their walk along the embankment overlooking the sea, each occupied with their own thoughts. Using the funicular railway they descend to the beach and to the town. The sea has a calming effect. The murmur of the waves’ ebb and flow conjures up thoughts of home. Susan recalls the times she spent on the beach at Westgate-on-Sea with her parents when a child. Interestingly they are allowed on this beach at Le Trèport but the Kent beaches are out of bounds: this, of course, might change should the Germans reach the French coast.

‘What does it say on the card Sister gave you?’ inquires Doris.

‘The Hotel des Bains, I wonder where it’s located?’

‘It’s not far from here, I’ll show you.’

‘How do you know? … Oh, I forgot. Captain Herbert Good MC must have shown you.’

‘That he did, and on more than one occasion.’

Susan is unnecessarily concerned about booking the room, as it turns out. She doesn’t want Matron to find out; she expresses this concern to Doris who laughs. ‘You don’t think she checks all the hotel registers do you. If you’re so worried that you’ll be found out, why don’t you book it in his name? I don’t suppose his commanding officer will check where he’s been and besides if it is in his name, he’ll have to pay.’

‘I wasn’t thinking about that, but I suppose you’re right, it’s usually the male – I nearly said husband – who pays the bill.’ They both laugh at the thought.

The hotel is very clean and appears comfortable. They are welcomed by a little, bespectacled lady. Susan thinks she looks a little fierce, but this may well have been due to her own nervousness. It is assumed that she is the proprietor. *Bonjour Madam, Comment allez-vous?’* the hotelier asks with a smile. The greeting, although pleasant, does nothing to calm Susan’s nerves. In her excitement over planning this day with James she has overlooked the fact that she may have to speak in French. Support is needed but is nowhere to be found, Doris has quietly nipped off to the *toilette*. So, in halting French she has no option but to swallow hard and carry on – somehow. She had not studied French at school but has picked up a few words while working in France, and has taken the precaution of learning a phrase or two which she attempted to commit to memory. '*Enchantè madam, Avez-vous* … er … *des* … er … *chambres?'* The lady looks long and hard at Susan, who by this time is beginning to perspire with embarrassment. Then, having witnessed Susan's dilemma, her face lights up and she grins broadly. 'How many night you stay?' she says in halting English. Her accent, in another context may sound amusing, however it is clearly understandable. 'Er … just the one, in the name of Lieutenant James Hemmings.' Details are taken. 'You are a nurse?' 'Yes madam.' '*Ah... ange de pitie"* replies Madam. Normally a deposit is payable but the hotelier feels a frisson of likeable pity for the young English girl, she therefore decides to forgo this charge. It is only for one night, and anyway, the man will pay.

'*Chambre, numèro cinq.'*

'Merci madam.'

'Thank you, *au revoir.'*

Once outside the hotel Susan takes a deep breath. Turning to Doris she demands, ‘Where were you when I needed you?’

‘I don’t speak French m’dear. I always left it up to Herbert.’

‘Oh God, I didn’t ask for a double room. She may think it is just for him and give us a single bed.’

‘So, what’s the problem m’dear,’ says Doris laughing. ‘I’m sure she knew. You couldn’t confuse anyone, even if you tried. You’re too innocent.’

Now, mission accomplished, the pair chat and giggle on their way along the beach and back to the funicular railway. Once up on the coastal path Susan asks, ‘How are we going to get back to Etaples?’ ‘No problem, m’dear. There isn’t any need to worry. There’s constant hospital traffic between Le Trèport and the camp at Etaples.’

All that remains for Nurse Susan Cooper is the counting off of the days until she will meet James. Prior to her ‘outing today’, she had spelt out her plans to her fiancée and told him that she would only contact him between now and the date of assignation should anything untoward happen. Please God, she prays, there will not be an unexpected major military push within the next seven days.

The next morning Susan is informed by Matron that she is to be transferred from the medical to the surgical wing. Not in itself a problem, she thinks, except that the shift pattern and schedule may change, in which case the yearned for romantic tryst will have to be cancelled. Susan now feels anxious and quite depressed.

Her first day working in the theatre turns out to be more of a trial than expected. She is used to applying dressings to weeping, seeping and bloody wounds but is unprepared for the brutality of the operating theatre. It is a busy time. The Canadian hospital is overrun with casualties from the previous battle at Vimy Ridge and the General Hospital is dealing with not only the British wounded, but also other colonial troops. Therefore there is more than the usual number of operations being carried out, hence the drafting in of experienced nurses such as Susan Cooper.

The Canadian trooper is placed on the operating table in order to have his left leg amputated. What remains of his leg, the stump just above the knee, is shredded with the thigh bone protruding. 'Hold the stump', orders the surgeon to Susan. This she does. It isn't a pleasant sight but she copes. The surgeon takes up the saw in his right hand. The scraping sound and sight of saw on bone is the last thing Susan remembers. On coming round she goes to sit on a chair outside. 'Don't worry nurse, you're not the first and you won't be the last one to faint. You'll get used to it', says the male medical orderly.

True enough, given the number of amputations, she becomes accustomed to thc severance of limbs. However, it isn't easy to ignore the fact that there is the possibility of seeing someone she knows on that operating table. These thoughts make it more imperative to make sure she is free to see James before anything terrible can happen to him. A visit to Sister Bridget's office is required. The fact that this Sister furnished Susan with the details of the hotel, indicates that she understands the significance of what Susan has planned.

'Well, how is the surgical nursing going Nurse Hemmings?'

'I'm coping now, although I did pass out on the first occasion.'

'I know. I heard about it and if it's any consolation, so did I. But that's not what you are here about, is it?'

'No, what I really …'

'No need to explain. I've had a word with the Sister in surgical and you will get your pass, so relax. The Vimy Ridge conflict appears to have abated. But remember what I said. Do not let Matron hear about what you have organised.'

She assures Sister Bridget that she won't. There is a second reason for feeling relieved and rejoicing that day. Her father, Harry, has written informing her of his pending leave during which time he hopes to move house; her mother has found a more modern and larger property for possible rent.

Just five days to go now before she will be happier still.

CHAPTER TWENTY-FOUR

Sergeant Harry Cooper scans the horizon from the upstairs portal in the loft of what remains of a war-torn barn. He can hear the rumblings of battle in the far distance; small plumes of smoke rise here and there indicating an intermittent barrage is in progress. But it is the middle distance that holds his attention. There still remain long wooded ridges with dry (thank God) hillsides. The spring months with the incessant rain has allowed the vegetation, temporarily dormant, to burgeon again, and a thin verdant carpet spreads across the area; a welcome change from glutinous brown mud.

Harry tries to wipe the scene of the quagmire and carnage of last year's Somme battlefield from his mind. The new green vegetation reminds him of home, of the East Kent Downs. Thoughts conjure up visions of Beryl, her fair hair bundled up on her head, kept in place with a scarf; busying herself around their home cooking; the smell of newly prepared pancakes in his nostrils. He's just received her latest letter in which she informs him of the possibility of moving house. 'Three bedrooms' are needed she says, 'one for us, one for Susan and one for Charlie.' But what to do when Susan gets married he muses. They can't accommodate James as well if she eventually has a child. He contemplates the possibilities and realises the solution is, reluctantly, for the Hemmings to take responsibility in this respect: it is normal in Harry's experience for the daughter to be with her parents at the time of the birth, particularly for the first born, and Beryl would certainly want to have Susan at their home. The need of moving to bigger and better accommodation becomes an imperative: Harry's inability to help is a persistent thought and worry to him. 'I hope my coming leave allows me time to help moving house' he tells his pal, Sergeant-major Boneaply. That bridge will eventually have to be crossed, in the meantime he needs to get safely through the week and then it's off, back to the shaws, valleys and hop fields of home.

Harry is also concerned about the cost of moving house. Beryl assures him that there is no need to be worried; they have, she writes, had an unexpected windfall. She refrains from telling him more: the news will be a surprise when he gets home.

Harry watches idly as an aeroplane advances skywards across the fields towards the enemy lines, the co-pilot armed with a camera; it is presumably on reconnaissance, he wonders if James is the pilot, or the cameraman. As it nears the area being pounded, puffs of smoke appear as if by magic around the aircraft. It is no fun being in the trenches but Harry thinks it slightly more appealing than being in a flimsy wooden contraption up in the sky. At least if he is hit, the chances of receiving help are better; for a pilot, once hit, there is little chance of being rescued; unlike the enemy airmen, British pilots are not issued with parachutes. Harry admires James but can't understand why he wants to fly.

He hopes, but does not expect, to be present at James and Susan's wedding. The meetings with James have been infrequent but pleasant affairs. He likes the lad, he is kind and polite, the perfect match for his daughter. Although obviously middle class he is at home in the Cooper's house. 'There are', Harry said to his wife, 'no airs and graces about him'. Any abrasive social edges have, he assumes, been knocked off when the lad worked in the factory; besides his father comes from working class stock. Perhaps this is why Harry gets on so well with Gordon – inferences and nuances are understood. Gordon's wife Moira is different, but then life is full of compromises. He has no problem with her, although Beryl still thinks Moira is 'a bit of a social snob.'

Harry's quiet moment is interrupted by the booming voice of the Sergeant-major: 'Over here gentlemen.'

Senior NCOs and officers gather around Captain East in the dimly lit basement of the derelict farm house. They all stand to attention when the Colonel arrives.

The ensemble listen intently to the commander's briefing. He is almost apologetic about the paucity of facts; this is no surprise to some of those present as it is not unusual for HQ to keep the PFI (poor bloody infantry) in the dark as to what is about to happen. 'Fluidity of movement is what is required; expect the unexpected,' the Colonel is keen on repeating.

The irony of the Colonel's warning was illustrated in the divisional theatre concert Harry attended recently. On centre stage was a mud trench wall and on one side stood a German, on the other a British soldier. The Tommy was holding up a trench periscope so that the German soldier could use the mirror for the purposes of shaving. The sketch was titled 'In the trenches 1957!' The joke was not lost on the audience, or on the attending General: clearly no one expects much movement for the foreseeable future.

The Colonel's briefing is however more comprehensive than usual. The Generals, they are informed, have decided that attacking on a broad-front is only partially successful. The Canadians have now totally secured Vimy Ridge but the British and Australian gains in the south are minimal. The tactic is now to be changed to small-scale operations over an area of about eleven miles.

The Colonel's purpose in calling together all his company and platoon commanders, and their senior NCOs is to explain the new innovative ideas, and to ensure everyone is 'singing from the same hymn sheet'. Occasionally in the past, messages passed down the line are lost in interpretation – rather like when playing a game of Chinese whispers.

The Royal Engineers Pioneer Battalion from New Zealand and a battalion of British Bantams have dug numerous tunnels through the chalky soil under the city of Arras. And it is from these tunnels that Harry, his platoon and hundreds of other troops will launch the ground attack. So extensive is this system that two sorts of tunnels have been dug, one for the movement of troops, the other sort as tramways for transporting ammunition and evacuating casualties.

On emerging from the tunnels the allied troops will advance in open formation says the Colonel, 'with lines of troops leapfrogging each other, thus allowing them time to re-group before advancing forward. All this will be done while moving forward under a creeping barrage.' This he adds, as if they needed telling, 'requires a lot of careful rehearsal.'

Sergeant Harry Cooper is pleased to be included with the planning at this stage of a battle as it makes a change from being kept in the dark. He is also pleased to get the opportunity to chat to his old friend Mossey, now a Sergeant. They have served together since the beginning of 1916. And they have progressed in parallel through the ranks, and now, after eighteen months at the Front, are considered experienced veterans; they are aware however that the odds of surviving this war decreases with each battle. The one bit of good news conveyed by the Colonel is the entry of the United States into the war, but their actual appearance on the battlefield will, of necessity, take some time. Nevertheless, it is good to know, opined Moz that the allied forces will outnumber the enemy eventually, which, hopefully, will hasten the end.

The meeting is over, and the two pals take the opportunity to have a more personal chat.

‘What yer going to do after the war Harry, assuming we’re still standing at the end?’

‘I don’t rightly know Moz. I know it seems strange, but I’ve got used to working full-time,’ he says, laughing cynically. ‘You know, I’ve never been better off financially. Everyone in my family is working, even young Charlie has a job and is now contributing to our budget.’

‘Blimey Harry! You’re not saying you want this bloody war to go on, are yer?’

‘No, course not. It’s just that I’ve become used to always being on the very bottom rung … you know … always taking orders.’

‘Yer still taking orders, Harry.’

‘I know but I’ve sort of enjoyed the responsibility of being a platoon Sergeant, like you. I don’t fancy going back to being a Private. Do you?’

‘Gawd, No! Who wants to be paid less … I know what yer mean Harry. But they don’t ‘ave sergeants in civvy street, unless you want to be a copper.’

‘Gordon Hemmings has offered me a job, come the end, as a supervisor. But will the gunpowder factory still be operating after the war?’

‘I don’t want to be a pessimist, but aren’t yer – pardon the pun – jumping the gun? We might reach the end before anyone else!’

‘And what about you Moz, what do you intend doing?’

‘I ain't got no plans. I was offered a foreman’s job before I was conscripted. But I don’t know if my old firm still exists. The only thing I want to do is get home after this latest fracas, see the wife and see my baby daughter christened.’

‘You’ll make it Moz.’

Moz may appear to some as a rough diamond with his squat broad frame and broken nose – due to bouts in the ring as an amateur boxer. He fulfils the ‘wide boy’ image of the East End petty criminal to a T. But he has a heart of gold. Harry remembers the time he saw him crying on receiving the news of the birth of his daughter. He’s only seen her once since then. Still, there is only a week to go before the planned-for leave; provided the latest sortie doesn’t prolong things.

Following the briefing, the next day and a half is taken up with the rehearsals. Single lines of British and Australian soldiers are assembled behind mock sap heads; on a given signal they ‘emerge’ from these and fan out into line. Subsequent platoons leapfrog the one in front in the manner dictated, re-grouping before moving through the next line and so on. Officers with white arm bands move at a speed simulating the advance behind a creeping barrage; whether or not this practice will work remains to be seen. At least the troops can see the purpose of it, and it is a change from charging blindly over the top.

On the eve of the battle Sergeant Harry Cooper follows his platoon commander at the rear down into a tunnel. Behind him comes Sergeant Mossy with his platoon. The Royal Engineer tunnellers, aided in this section by a regiment of little Bantams – so called because of their below average stature – they are rightly looking pleased with their work. The Bantams look as though they belong there. They scurry about like creatures from another world, issuing ammunition, handing out Mills bombs to designated personnel, bringing down stretchers for the medics. Occasionally they tap a man on the arm as if to say, 'good luck' and grin. The grins are supposed to be a sign of encouragement and support but in the candle-lit narrow conduits the Bantams appear like sinister troglodytes: they give the scene a frightengly surreal quality.

Harry has become aware of one young man in particular. He is Private Tim Gibson, a slightly built lad who, like some of the other younger soldiers, is under age; he reminds Harry of another youngster in his family's care, Charlie. Like Charlie he has no parents. In this case the difference being that Gibson is an orphan and never knew his mother or father; he joined the Army in order to get away from the brutality of his orphanage: out of the frying pan into the fire – literally. Harry notices that the lad appears to be growing increasingly agitated in the stuffy underground chamber; he could be suffering from claustrophobia. He knows the lad isn't one to funk it – he's been over the top twice before – but he is sweating profusely and there is the risk he'll lose control and go berserk, which will prove extremely tricky in a confined space. Each has his own way of handling the stress, of conquering or at least coping with fear. Harry moves a junior

NCO in position next to the young lad with instructions to keep an eye on him.

Captain East forbids anyone to smoke; if he hadn't, the foul smelling atmosphere, the increased coughing, the spewing of phlegm and fear creating body odour, would be vomit inducing, this is not to say it isn't for one or two soldiers.

The extensive construction of the wood and corrugated tin-lined catacombs gives a temporary and totally delusionary sense of security; the tunnel looks sturdy and bomb proof. Alas this sense of safety is short-lived. The engineer officer explains that whilst they may have some protection from above, they have none from the side. The Bosh, he tells the infantrymen, 'have also dug tunnels and are listening for movement, which if detected, could prove fatal' – the officer reminds them to keep quiet. The fact that there is no way out should the enemy break through or cause the tunnel to collapse, adds to the soldiers' unease. Most of the infantry is used to fighting in the open or in a trench, but not in the more constricted space of a tunnel. The feeling of confined tension multiplies as time passes; the sooner they emerge out onto the battlefield the better.

The previous issue of rum helps calm the nerves in some but stokes the fire of aggression in others.

There is no whistle, no shouting. The platoon commander, Lieutenant Markus Jones, a fresh faced youth compared with Harry – indeed with most of the platoon – is their immediate leader. Not that his age is of concern, but more of a worry is his lack of experience: public school, and into the Army – at nineteen he's still in his teens. He comes to check with Harry that all is OK at the rear. He is likeable but has no idea how to deal with people. The men laugh, but not to his face, at his adolescent enthusiasm. 'OK chaps! All together now, let's do the business,' he says, as if supporting his school football team. 'We're right behind you, sir' someone would reply in a mocking tone. Things have not been the same since Lieutenant Laurence Griffith bought it; the men enjoyed the latter's theatrical humour. He had completed his university education and was thus a couple of years older than Jones, which made all the difference.

On a hand signal passed down the line the men stand up. On command they fix bayonets and turn right before shuffling forward. The nearer they get to the tunnel's entrance the louder the noise. Fusillades of shells from the guns provide the barrage that passes overhead. Emerging into the bleak dawn light is akin to jumping into a pool of icy water: it is a shock. Eyes blink against the sudden light, the cold wind chills and cuts through clothing, the noise is deafening. The men spread out into line, kneel and wait until the last man, Sergeant Harry Cooper, is ready to give the order to move forward. They soon stop and the next line containing

Sergeant Mossy, move ahead of them, and so the leapfrogging continues until the company commander indicates it is time to charge. Then the barrage ceases.

Like adrenaline-fuelled screaming banshees they run towards the enemy, some collapsing on impact under enemy fire. The entangled barbed wire causes problems for many but once over or through, the men plunge into the German trench. Fighting is hand-to-hand, frantic, bloody and vicious. With the aid of mills bombs and thrusting bayonets the objective is secured: it took just twenty minutes of murderous combat to complete this phase.

Sergeant Harry Cooper tells the men to secure their positions in the trench and remain alert for any counter-attack and sniper fire. A traverse along the trench reveals the body of young Lieutenant Markus Jones. He lies face down in the muddy channel still clasping his revolver. He hasn't survived his first real battle. No doubt his fellows will remember him; he will be included in *The Times* list of the fallen and his name will appear on a public school memorial: what a bloody waste of a good life, thinks Harry, before calling for a stretcher party.

Eventually another line of fresh troops move forward to take charge of the newly acquired trench. Harry and his boys trudge back. His job is not yet done. With the young platoon commander dead, it is his task to count the casualties and report to the company commander.

On reaching the temporary company HQ that evening he meets Sergeant-major Boneaply; he hands him the accounted names of those still alive.

'Here you are sir, better give this to Captain East' says Harry.

'That won't be necessary, Harry.'

'What do you mean?'

'I'll keep it until we are designated a new commander.'

'Not Captain East as well?'

'I'm afraid so.'

'So who's taken over the company and the platoon?'

Boneaply looks at Harry with a knowing deadpan face. 'You've heard of a field commission, have you?' Harry stands to attention and salutes Boney who, he presumes, is the newly assigned Lieutenant Boneaply, now platoon commander. Given the circumstances Harry is pleased by the new appointment.

‘Congratulations is not the right word,’ says Harry, ‘but I’ll be proud to serve under you, sir.’

‘Nice of you to say that Harry, but I want you to recommend someone to take your place. You, Harry, are the new acting company Sergeant-major. You’re taking my place.’

‘Why me? Sergeant Mossey is senior to me. He’s the most experienced of the senior NCOs; he should be the next Sergeant-major.’

‘He was Harry. Now it’s you.’

‘Oh! No, not Moz, as well!’ Harry sits down with a thump, his head clasped in his hands. He feels sick to the pit of his stomach. He’d lost his cousin, then Ciggie and the likeable platoon commander amongst many others, but Sergeant Mossy was his ‘best mate’, they’d come through the Somme – the worse of all hells – they’d fought in the battle for Vimy Ridge and other conflicts, shared personal and family secrets; they were truly ‘brothers in arms’; he’d started with and wanted to end it all with him: it took some time for him to compose himself, but he had to, as the new platoon commander Lieutenant Boneaply reminded him – ‘you’re the Company Sergeant-major now.’

Boney pats Harry’s shoulder and invites him to share the remains of his secreted bottle of whiskey, an invitation Harry accepts with alacrity. They briefly talk about those who have departed before Boney reminds Harry of the burial service. As company Sergeant-major he will have a role to play in mustering the remaining troops. He, Lieutenant Boneaply, platoon commander, needs to talk to the padre, the Colonel and the company second-in-command – a new company O.C. has not, as yet, been appointed. It is necessary to organise the burial party and a parade. This isn't the send-off the company wants before they depart for Blighty, but all agree it needs to be done. They can't just depart without first attending a memorial service, and bidding a heartfelt farewell to their comrades.

Members from a Chinese labour battalion have worked non-stop for two days, digging the graves and, although not Christian, they have erected the wooden crosses for the tombs.

The British and Australian soldiers form a square around the burial ground. The two commanding officers read out the names of the fallen prior to the padre, who, with due dignity, conducts the service. Harry finds it difficult not to respond when Moz's name is called out. As the newly-installed company sergeant-major he is fighting to keep inner feelings in check; his throat constricts, he bites his tongue, he feels his eyes filling up: it's not easy. He is also concerned for the young man who was near to panicking in the tunnel: he needn't worry; the lad stands there stony-faced without a flicker of emotion. Perhaps the lack of time he has spent with the company means he hasn't cemented any close relationships; or perhaps he is displaying the first signs of shell-shock. As is often the case, the heralding of the Last Post by the bugler releases the emotional safety catch and tears are seen to flow from a number of those present.

The atmosphere following the service is sombre; the very thought of going home does not, cannot, relieve the pain of losing close friends. Harry knows he has a duty to perform once he gets home: to go and see Moz's widow and their infant, not a duty he is looking forward to.

CHAPTER TWENTY-FIVE

Susan is finding it difficult to contain her excitement. James is arriving tomorrow.

Doris is determined to go to Le Trèport with Susan. 'You don't have to come, you know,' says Susan with an air of irritation.

'Oh, but I must m'dear. I have spent weeks, nay, months, listening to you talking about your Lothario, and now you have got me so intrigued that I just have to take a look at him.

He's not a Lothario … he's my Romeo.'

‘Well, Juliet, m’dear; I want to see your Romeo.’

‘Oh; alright then.’ She couldn’t be angry with Doris for too long. She has been a real pal and didn’t she help her find the hotel.

‘I promise not to interfere, honest. I won’t act the voyeur and I’ll be fair in my assessment’ she says, laughing.

The truck rumbles its way along the northern route to the little seaside resort. Susan tries to encourage the driver to go a little quicker. ‘Am I to assume that as you want me to put my little trotter down and go faster, that this is not a duty call? Why are you in such a hurry, you got a special date or something, a secret tryst? Mind you, I expect he’s there waiting already. If you were my bird, I would be. What rank is he? Have you got your overnight bag?’

‘Enough of the questions; don’t be so cheeky, and keep your mind on the driving’ retorts Susan. Doris is finding the whole situation amusing, and can’t help but dissolve into a fit of the giggles.

The truck rounds the curve in the drive but before it reaches the main entrance, Susan commands the driver to stop. ‘We’ll get off here’, she says. ‘Good move girl’ replies the driver. ‘You don’t want to be spotted by matron.’ The thought of seeing matron at that moment made the nurses stop in their tracks and inadvertently look around. ‘Come on m’dear, too late to worry about that now. Where did you say you will meet him?’

‘Somewhere round here. Let’s walk down the drive away from the front door or people will be wondering what we want and what we are doing.’

It isn’t long before the warning honk from a truck’s horn is heard. The vehicle stops some thirty yards from the pair; the passenger is giving the driver instructions to carry on round the drive before exiting; from behind the cab steps a young Lieutenant from the RFC; a slim figure carrying a small valise. His stance and gait is familiar to Susan. She runs towards the subaltern and in her enthusiasm to embrace, knocks the hat from his head when throwing her arms about him.

Doris stands at an unobtrusive distance from the scene. She notes that he is of average height, has dark wavy hair with lean features. His youthful shoulders are broad and he walks with a confident gait, although he looks a little tired, probably come off a sortie last night. His whole demeanour changes when he gets within touching range of Susan. His smile is broad and his eyes glisten on seeing her. He is, thinks Doris, ‘a bloody good catch’. She is thrilled for her friend, and if she is to be honest to herself, a 'tad' jealous.

Susan, now arm in arm with James, leads her beau towards Doris. 'James, here is my best friend Doris. Doris this is my fiancée,' says Susan proudly.

'My, haven't you've done well m'dear!' replies Doris, offering her hand.

'I've heard so much about you,' says James, 'that I feel a handshake is inadequate' and kisses her on the cheek.

'He's a charmer as well, m'dear,' retorts a blushing and giggling Doris before adding, 'I must be going.'

'Won't you have tea with us Doris?' asks James.

'No, certainly not! Time is precious, m'dear. Goodbye.' With that she scoots off towards the main entrance to the hospital.

'Have you found us somewhere to stay, my darling?' inquires James.

'Yes, but let's walk along the cliff path first. It reminds me so much of home.'

There is little talk of the war. The theme is home, the major subject is the longed for wedding. 'My mother wants us to have the reception at our house, but I don't think some of the guests from the factory will be comfortable there. Besides which, she will see it as her domain and in her way will want to control everything – albeit it with good intentions', announces James.

'I know the best place and it is so symbolic of the meeting between your family and mine.' She jumps with joy at the very thought of celebrating in Mr and Mrs Parting's hotel at Westgate-on-Sea. 'It will be perfect! What do you think James?'

'Oh, yes. And Mrs Parting can entertain us all after the meal with her renderings on the pianoforte.' They laugh at the thought and walk on towards the funicular railway, and descend to the town centre of Le Trèport.

The proprietor, Madam Du Pont, is there to welcome them. She insists on taking Susan's small attaché case and leads them upstairs to the attic room. Seeing Susan's look of concern at being given what, surely, must be the smallest bedroom in the house, Madam Du Pont allays her guest's fears by explaining that it is the one with the best view and the most privacy.

The room, given the vagaries of war and the difficulty of obtaining or replacing the niceties of decoration, is adequate. 'Look a double-bed, James. I thought for one horrible minute it would be two singles.' Opposite the door there is a small chest of drawers, upon which stands a folding mirror. There are no curtains but the window has sturdy shutters. To the left of the bed there is a small wardrobe and by its head a delicate small table with a single rose laid beside a candle and holder, complete with taper. 'I think Madam Du Pont is an absolute brick … don't you James?' James couldn't agree more. They turn to thank her but she has surreptitiously disappeared.

Extricating himself from another gripping embrace James has to tell Susan that 'I don't want to seem unromantic but I've not had anything to eat since breakfast.'

'Not to worry my darling. Doris and I, in true army fashion, did a 'recce' and we found a nice little restaurant. We shall go there *tout de suite*.'

The walk back along the shore from the restaurant to the hotel is pleasant. The off-shore breeze is warm and the sea air is sweetly pungent in the evening twilight. Their path is illuminated by the rising full-moon, a welcome change for James from the flares lighting up the battlefields and, thankfully, a lot quieter.

Back at the hotel the candle is left unlit, the night is balmy, the shutters remain open. In a fit of abandoned passion clothes are discarded in a frantic haste. Arms wrap around and clutch in fierce embrace as lips smother each other with an intense desire. Months of wanton absence is gratified. Feelings of exuberant joy and love become totally consuming as they lie enveloped in the light of a white moon beam. A passing dark cloud withdraws upward revealing Susan's blond hair, her eyes shine, lips are pressed against his cheek.

James nuzzles her neck.

The dawn chorus heralds a new day. The first of many together hopes James as he contmplates his future wife. A tress of hair cascades down her cheek, the slightly turned up nose and gentle features hold his attention; he can feel the warmth of her body: shivers of pleasure are evident. He absorbs her aroma: it is intoxicating. Sensing his attention Susan nestles closer, tilts her head and their pleached limbs promps Susan to entreat James to love her again.

Remaining feelings of exuberant joy, intimacy, and love are totally consuming as they lie there enveloped in the embracing light of the white moon.

Later a gentle, almost polite, tap on the door is heard and Madam Du Pont informs them that it is ten o'clock in the morning, and asks if they would like breakfast. The reply is in the affirmative, and following a quick wash and dress they appear downstairs in the dining room.

Madam greets them with, '*Bonjour Romeo et Juliet'*. They return the smile, by now too committed to each other to feel any embarrassment at such comments. All the other guests have departed some time ago. After breakfasting on coffee and crisp rolls, James pays the bill and thanks the proprietor for everything. He shakes her hand in a polite English manner, while Susan is pleasantly taken aback when madam kisses her on both cheeks in a nice French sort of way.

The trail back up to the cliff top is slow and increasingly sad. Neither want this time to end; when will they meet again: *will* they met again? James of course has to return to his squadron and his aircraft, and Susan to the more depressing scenes at the hospital in Etaples.

CHAPTER TWENTY-SIX

Susan is looking forward eagerly to returning to England; her interest will inevitably be focussed on the preparation for their wedding; whenever that will be. At present she is completing her duties with, according to Doris, an air of unusual gaiety. That is until Sister Bridget calls her into the office. 'Judging by your happy demeanour you had a really good time Nurse,' says Sister eyeing her with a knowing look.

'Yes Sister, I can honestly say that I did. But why am I here, have I done something wrong?'

‘Not to my mind, but I must tell you that Matron wishes to see you.’

‘Oh! Goodness … What’s it about, do you know?’

‘Alas, I don’t. On a scale of one to ten, I’d say it was a seven. Had it been higher she would have demanded to see you A.S.A.P. I can’t tell you any more than that, so ‘good luck’ and let me know how you get on.’

Doris has an enigmatic look, and has to ask Susan why she is spending so much time adjusting her uniform this morning.

‘I’ve been summoned to see the Welsh dragon.’

‘Oh, really, what have you done m’dear?’

‘As far as I’m concerned, I don’t know … nothing at all.’

‘Do you remember the cheeky driver saying something about being seen by matron the other day? I wonder if you’ve been spotted by her or one of her spies … how exciting, you must let me know what happens, m’dear.’

‘I’m glad you find it entertaining … well, I’m off … wish me luck.’

A summons, full of power and foreboding emanates from the office. The dragon has a voice of a lower register, at least an octave below that of a normal woman. It is guaranteed to put the wind up any nurse, and sister or doctor for that matter. Susan buckles at the knees slightly and advances with small steps towards the large desk. Matron, as seems to be the custom of those in charge, continues to concentrate on the papers in front of her, thus giving the impression that the interviewee is of secondary importance.

'Do you remember what I told you when you first arrived here Nurse Cooper?'

'Yes matron, you said we have to be disciplined and dedicated. And I think I have fulfilled those criteria.'

'Oh, do you now! I also warned you about fraternizing with the patients, both officers and other ranks.'

'But I have not been fraternizing with any patients, Matron.'

'So who was he? Someone you picked-up while ambling through the streets of Le Trèport?'

Susan was determined to make the dragon work for the answers, and she certainly wasn't going to apologise for being with James. 'It is true Matron. I did amble through the streets of Le Trèport. And before you ask, yes I did stay the night at a hotel with the young man who accompanied me through the streets.'

'This young officer is required to concentrate on fighting a war, be it on the ground, or in this case as I understand it, in the air. Diversions of an intimate nature may well distract him and lives may be put at risk. There may be times when his thoughts are, for better or worse, directed solely towards you.'

'Oh, I hope so Matron.'

'How long have you been walking out with this young man?'

'About two years, Matron.'

'And when will you be seeing him again?'

'When he comes home, and we get married.'

'I see. You know the Army disapproves of men serving with their spouses when on active service.'

'But he's not my spouse … yet.'

'Ah, so you are at the pre-nuptial state, known in the trenches as neurasthenia.'

‘I know what that means matron, and I am not nervously debilitated,’ retorts Susan with some indignity.

‘A spirited answer I must say. Well, there’s no point in sending you home as your tour of duty is due to end shortly. You’re dismissed.’

Susan crosses to the door feeling somewhat relieved. As her hand clasps the door handle Matron stops her. Susan could detect something approaching a grin, but she couldn’t be sure and then Matron spoke. ‘I wish you luck for the future Nurse Cooper, I hope you’ll both be very happy.’

‘Tell me. What did she say?’ asks Doris. ‘Did the dragon breathe fire, m’dear?’

‘No, it was more of a warm glow … I think she wanted to let me know that nothing escapes her.’

CHAPTER TWENTY-SEVEN

Remedial treatment is not restricted to the medical wards or the convalescent hospitals. A third mode of recuperative treatment, and one much welcomed by patients and staff, are the concerts, both civilian and military. On alternate Saturdays the YMCA hut is filled to the brim with an eager audience for the afternoon matinee and the evening show.

During the Battle of the Somme theatre entertainment had been suspended but it has returned this year and everyone agrees that the remedial effect of laughter acts as a necessary tonic. The medics are of the opinion that it aids recovery.

In a base camp the size of Etaples there is no problem obtaining musicians. British, Canadian and Australian bandsmen combine to form an orchestra; today's pianist is recognised as the Private who comes to practice most days in the canteen. The repertoire is a change from the classics he played previous, but he is equally at home playing jazz and modern music. Alternate shows are put on by the military personnel and civilian concert parties.

Susan and Doris hurry along to the evening performance, the house is packed. The first half consists of two one-act plays: first, Gertrude Jennings', *The Bathroom Door* followed by J M Barrie's *The Twelve Pound Look.* But it is the second half of the show that is especially enjoyed by those whose main theatrical experience is the music hall – that is, the majority of the audience. The comedian with his 'low' jokes and digs at authority make the rafters shake with their laughter. The chorus of the popular songs are delivered by the four hundred testosterone-fuelled voices of the audience. The trilling rendition from the nurses is at times drummed out, but they don't mind. The collective rendering of the finale is different: it evokes an emotional poignancy that is deeply moving. For the final number the house lights come up and the atmosphere changes completely, there is a collective sentiment aptly expressed. The casts assemble on stage and the pianist begins to play, and everyone sings *The Long, Long Trail.*

There's a long, long trail a-winding
Into the land of my dreams,
Where the nightingales are singing,

The deep rhythmic melancholic sound of the male voices is almost unbearable to Susan. The rendition makes even the most war-hardened throat constrict. And for one particular member of the audience the following line,

And a white moon beams ...

evokes the most heartfelt of recent memories. At the end of the song Doris asks, 'And where were you m'dear ... methinks, back in Le Trèport?' It was then that Susan realises that her arms are wrapped tightly around her body in a self-embrace. She looks around in embarrassment but no need to worry as most of the audience is making efforts to exit the auditorium, except she catches Sister Bridget and Matron smiling in a knowing way – they look away quickly.

'Not long now m'dear, what are you plans?'

‘First thing is to take a break, reacquaint properly with my mum and Charlie, before contacting the hospital and resuming work. I hope by the time I get home we will have moved house, otherwise I’ll be helping to do this. And most importantly, I’ll bc assisting in the planning of my wedding. I just hope that the wait for James coming home is not too long. What about you?’

‘I’ll probably stay here and meet a nice army doctor and when the war is over, retire to the country and settle down and produce loads of kids. Actually I don’t know, but then none of us do. But I’ll miss you m’dear, you’ve been great fun, and …’

‘Stop there before you make me cry. I’ll really miss you Doris and when you’re on leave and when this beastly war is over we must … we will … get together again. But, hey, I’m not going home for another week.’

CHAPTER-TWENTY-EIGHT

Sergeant-major Cooper and Lieutenant Boneaply sit together on the deck of the home-bound vessel watching the coast of France disappear over the horizon. The calming effect of the moonlight playing a shimmy-like dance on the rippling waves goes unnoticed. It ought to be a joyous time. ‘We’re going home, why aren’t we happy, sir?’ asks Harry.

‘Simple. Each time we go home indicates that we have spent a longer and longer time at the Front. And this means the odds of survival are getting proportionally less and less.’

‘Blimey, that’s a pessimistic view. You mean the cup of fortune is half empty; the optimist would see it as being half full.’

‘Yes, and isn’t that the way we used to see it. Weren’t we pleased to go home with an extra stripe on our arm, so to speak? It’s been rapid promotion, and why? Dead man’s shoes Harry, that’s why. If we carry on at this rate by the end of next year I could be a Colonel and you’ll be a company commander or alternatively …’ He taps his thigh in a gesture of recognition that they have come to the end of the point of this discussion.

The pair remain temporarily silent; there isn’t anything else to add.

The white cliffs signify the end of the return journey. The port of Folkestone is, as usual, bustling with hundreds of soldiers, coming and going between the railway station and the port. Boney nudges Harry and points to a group of very young looking Tommys. They are smart and sprightly with eager young faces. ‘Who are they Harry?’

‘That’s the new company of optimists, sir’.

‘Oh, yes. Well, we had better gather our old company of pessimists together and march them to the station. Our old company,’ says Harry laughing derisively ‘you can’t call young Tim Gibson old, but compared to that lot he’s a veteran. How comc he joined up when he is under age?’

‘He ran away from his orphanage. He wasn’t happy. He was getting bullied; I think he saw the Army as a means of escape: would you believe that!’

‘Or perhaps he sees it as a way of ending it all. Poor little beggar. I can’t help but feel sorry for him’, says Harry shaking his head. ‘Where’s he spending his leave?’

‘I think one of the lads has taken pity on him and he’s staying with his family,’ concludes Lieutenant Boneaply.

They then shake hands and Sergeant-major Cooper smartly salutes the Lieutenant.

‘Have a good one Harry. See you in a week or so.’

The train chugs on up the coast in a northerly direction: Deal, Ramsgate, Broadstairs, Margate and then Harry’s stop, Westage-on-Sea. Alighting from the train he looks at the tidy shops under the glass and metal canopy and wonders whether or not to enter the florist and purchase a bouquet. But he decides carrying a kit bag and a rifle is enough. Turning left he trundles down the hill and out to the edge of town. As before, on reaching the top of the hill facing down to the depressing looking house he calls home, he stops. Instead of his pace gathering momentum as in the past, he maintains a steady trudge to the front door.

Susan won't be there, she is still in France. There'll be no over excited hugs. Beryl will, of course, be pleased to see him. But she, being of a more reserved nature, will save her overt enthusiasm for later; as it is, it's Charlie who comes to the door.

'Hello Uncle,' he says with a grin, 'let me carry yer rifle.'

'Yes, and when you've deposited that, come back for the kitbag, and then put the kettle on while I say hello to me wife.' With that he throws his hat onto a chair and unbuckles his webbing, which, with a shrug of the shoulders, he lets drop to the floor.'

Beryl enters the room while drying her hands on a towel. 'Harry darlin', come here and let me hug you.' After the usual felicitous greetings are over, during which time Charlie tactfully stays in the kitchen, before re-appearing around the corner. 'Anyone for tea?' he asks.

'Yes. You got that boy well trained Beryl. Which system did you use?'

‘The Harry Cooper system; I said if you don’t abide by the house rules the Sergeant-major will be down on you like a ton of bricks.’

‘It’s nice to know that I wield such power from so far away’.

To placate young Charlie the old soldier gives him a lesson (without ammunition) on loading and unloading the rifle, and how to ‘make safe’ by applying the safety catch, but he drew the line at showing him how to fix bayonets. ‘That’s enough weapon training for one day. Here’s a couple of bob, now hop it for a while.’

At first, true to the habit of all English people they talk about the weather. ‘Did it rain much where you were?’ inquires Beryl.

‘No more than here I expect, except we’ve got these long troughs to keep the water in. Yeah, they’re called bloody trenches.’

‘You aren’t suffering from trench foot, are you? It makes your feet rot, I’m told.’

‘There is a cure for it I’m told … you have to get your feet rubbed by a loving wife,’ he says laughing.

‘And what if I refuse to do it, what then?’

‘Er, excuse me. Nobody refuses an order from the Sergeant-major,’ replies Harry pulling his wife towards him before they kiss again.

All the while enjoying this banter Beryl is watching her husband closely. He seems tired, worn out – battle fatigue is how they describe it in the papers. The overtly bubbly enthusiasm that is normally there on re-connecting has partly evaporated; he has been unusually serious most of the time. Perhaps after a good meal he will feel reinvigorated; the quickest way to a man’s heart is through his stomach, isn’t that what they say?

The evening meal is over and tactile bonding has to be postponed until Charlie has retired to bed. To Beryl’s surprise Harry expresses his need, not for love and sex, but for sleep. ‘I’m sorry love, but I’m totally knackered, I’m going to bed early.’

‘That’s alright dear. I’ve chores to do. You go and get your head down, I’ll be up later.’

She listens to Harry wearily clambering up the stairs. He enters the bedroom, strips off and flops onto the bed. Alas, he cannot sleep. Lying there, dark thoughts tumble over and over in his mind; faces, people he won’t ever see again appear, disappear and re-appear. The darkness of the room is claustrophobic, a reminder of being down the tunnel prior to exiting, and facing the onslaught of rifle and machine gun fire. His stomach is churning over, he feels nauseous.

He sits up, swings his legs out of bed and pads naked across the room and draws the curtains. The white moonlight turns everything a variegated shade of grey. He stands at the window eyeing the scenery. Hedgerows curl away in the distance like extended rolls of barbed wire. Distant trees seem to move as if suspicious alien shadows are on night patrol. He slaps his face in an attempt to bring himself round, away from the battlefield and back to the green, now grey, moonlit fields of home. Harry returns to the bed, sighs deeply and closes his eyes in another attempt to relax.

Beryl, by way of not wanting to wake her husband, disrobes by the light of the moon. She dons her nightdress and slides into bed. She opts not to embrace him, not yet. She can't sleep either, so lies there studying the man she so relies on next to her. They've been married a long time, over twenty years. They got married because of the unexpected pregnancy, but they didn't care about what others thought. It was what they wanted; it just came earlier than was socially acceptable. His caring resilience was evident early on when she lost their infant boy. He has been her silent rock ever since.

He is thinner this time, the puffiness under the eyes more noticeable. He is breathing deeply and moving in a restless fashion. His head rolls from side to side, unfathomable moans emanating from his mouth. Should she wake him? No. Best not, she thinks. Isn't it dangerous to wake someone in the middle of a nightmare? She doesn't really know, and doesn't want to take the risk. Judging by his more exaggerated movements, that's what it is. She drifts off into a fitful sleep.

Harry cannot switch-off, even in the lassitude of slumber dreams merge into what seems reality:

The tabs open and jumping onto the stage is Lieutenant Laurence Griffiths. His muddy uniform is in contrast to his silk scarf and a top hat. He twirls the silver topped cane, executes a dance and addresses the audience. 'Welcome to the theatre, the Theatre of War. It's your three minute call. Beginners on stage ... Fix bayonets!' Harry is amused. 'Tonight and for one night only ... all together now, let's sing our hearts out for the last time ... "Goodbye, Goodbye ... Cheerio old chum ... Goodbye". The tabs slide close and the scene fades away.

Harry feels a loss, he is becoming depressed. Ahead resting on the fire step is the wooden ladder. He climbs and walks forward looking for someone else to rekindle his enthusiasm. Down there in the mud there's a face grinning at him, it has a cigarette butt stuck to its lower lip. 'Ciggie, Ciggie, how are you old son?'

He sees a mark on Ciggie's forehead. 'How's yer head?'
'I'm OK Harry, boy; it's the rest of me that's a mess.' Three feet away his torso is twitching like that of a headless chicken, blood gushing forth. 'Christ!' Harry wants to vomit and runs back along the trench.

'Where are you going Cousin Harry?' A discordant voice calls. 'I'm going home; I can't take much more of this.'
'When you get there say goodbye to Dolly for me, and look after our boy Charlie.'
'Of course I will.' With that George's head drops to his chest, exposing the hole in the back of his head and the body folds down into the flooded trench.

Harry edges along to the entrance to a bomb crater and peers over the top.
'Moz, thank God you're here.'
'Before I go Harry, do me a favour.'
'Yeah ... sure, anything, old mate.'
'Kiss my new baby girl for me ... I never had the chance to say good-bye, do it for me Harry... promise.'
'Moz, don't go, don't go!'

The wind howls across no man's land and in the distant greyness can be heard the mournful incantation of voices calling, 'mother, mother help me.'

'STRETCHER BEARERS, STETCHER BEARERS, OVER HERE!'
'What are you calling for Harry?' A dismembered voice shouts, 'they're all fucking dead.'

Beryl's slumber is violently interrupted by Harry kicking out. Her shin is feeling the blow. She shakes his left shoulder and the response is immediate. Harry's body jerks violently, his head now off the pillow, he's breathing heavily and small beads of sweat break out on his forehead.

Harry turns. He looks at Beryl his eyes staring, his expression one of surprise, shock even. 'Where am I?'

'It's alright Harry,' she whispers. 'You're at home, you're safe now. It's a nightmare, that's all; it's over now.' Beryl encircles him with her right arm, drawing him closer. Harry pulls down the top of her nightdress exposing her breasts and lays his head gently down. She listens to the short, sharp intakes of breath prior to feeling the dampness of his tears. She pulls him closer and worries that her loving husband, if hit often and hard enough, might eventually crack.

After a fraught and restless night's sleep Beryl slips quietly out of bed and makes her way downstairs. It is Sunday morning so there is no need for anyone to hurry. Charlie is already up and in the kitchen. 'Bless you Charlie, you've lit the fire and got the kettle on, thank you.'

'How is he, auntie?'

'Oh, he's fine. A bit tired. I think we ought to let him sleep.'

'He's not totally fine is he? I think he looks knackered and I heard him shouting, "Stretcher Bearers". What's his problem? Tell me auntie.'

'He had a bit of a nightmare. He said it's like in one of those new silent films that's on a loop, it keeps replaying. Charlie, I want you to do me and him a favour.'

'Anything to help my uncle Harry, what do yer want me to do?'

'Later today we are going to look at the 'new' house. Then we must move all our stuff and start on re-decorating the place. I know he's on leave and should be resting, but I think he needs to take his mind off the fighting and the killing. I think decorating the house, with your assistance, will help him to recover. What do you say, will you help?'

'Yeah, of course I will.'

'Don't ask him about the war. If he wants to talk, OK, but otherwise don't make the bad sights come back into his mind.'

‘Are you going to wake him?’

‘No, he’ll be down soon. Get me that pan and the bacon. His nostrils will start twitching when he smells this sizzling away, and he’ll soon be sitting at this table – don’t you worry.’

Within ten minutes a puffy and bleary-eyed Harry lurches into the kitchen-cum-dining-cum-living room. ‘I’m following the trail of the scent. It smells good. Morning, Charlie.’ Harry kisses his wife and plonks himself down at the table. He is clearly in a better mood. He appears his old jovial and smiling self. ‘Well, what’s on the agenda today?’

‘You and I are going to view our ‘new’ home so we had better start packing when you’ve finished your breakfast.’

‘I’m going out uncle, but I’ll be back to give you a hand moving.’

‘It might be a good idea to call at Gordon and Moira Hemming’s house later. They may want to discuss the wedding and possibly have additional news about Susan and James. ‘Do you think Gordon will lend us a truck from the Works? We can’t carry all our furniture on a handcart.’

‘Yes, I’m sure he will.’

‘I’ll drive - no need to borrow a driver.’

‘And it might be an idea to ask if Charlie can have a couple hours off, or finish early so he can give us a hand.’

‘Right, that’s settled then. I’ll get changed and we’ll be off. Are you going now Charlie?’

‘Yeah, bye, see you later.’

‘I’m sorry about last night luv. I didn’t mean to kick you and wake you up, it’s just that … well … you know.’

‘I understand Harry; you’ve no need to apologise. God knows you’ve been through enough. I just hope that in time you will get over it.’ The couple embrace.

‘I expect I will, but it might not be until this bloody war is over. In the meantime let’s go and look at this house. I hope it is as good as you say.’

‘I’m sure you’ll like it, Harry’.

‘I been meaning to ask, I know there are now four of us working, but where is the money coming from to buy a house?’

‘We can now afford the mortgage repayments; the deposit was paid by someone else’.

‘Really: who did that, for Gawd’s sake? We haven’t got a Fairy God Mother!’

‘You know young Charlie lost his mum in tragic circumstances at the factory; well, Gordon - Mr Hemmings, my boss - God bless him, paid the deposit’.

‘So how much do we owe him?’

‘Absolutely nothing’.

‘Nothing! I can’t believe it … You got to be kidding?’

‘He reckons as the tragedy happened in the firm’s time and on the firm’s premises, she, or her family, should receive some compensation.’

‘Well, bless my soul, miracles never cease’.

The couple stroll along the deserted streets – it being Sunday, most of the inhabitants of the town are either at church or having a lie in. They turn a corner and the pace quickens as they survey the row of Victorian terraced houses. ‘Which one is it?’ asks Harry. ‘Number 37,’ replies Beryl.

The house is much bigger than their present abode. Behind the waist high brick wall a tiled path, no more than three or four yards long, leads to a red door. The ground floor sitting room boasts a bay window, and seen through the window is a substantial fire place with tiled surround. On entering they are in a hallway that is marked by pretty matching patterned tiles, a continuation of the path leading to the front door. On the left is the parlour. The Coopers are impressed; their present abode has just one room which Beryl calls - the everything room - this is where they eat, read, sow and occasionally bathe in the metal tub. Next is the dining room with its red floor slabs which extend into the kitchen; the latter has a large Belfast sink and a coal-fired iron range for cooking. There is storage space under the stairs. Charlie returns briefly, scouts around outside in the yard and comes back excitedly exclaiming ‘we got a toilet that flushes’; no more trotting down to the privy at the end of the garden; he then scuttles off to get the train to Faversham and returns to work. Susan, when informed, is particularly delighted to know there are three bedrooms upstairs, ‘one each’ she says delightedly.

‘What do you think Harry? Does it pass muster?’

‘Brilliant. And I like a garden with enough space to put a shed at the end for me tools and storage. You did well to find this.’

‘I hate to say this, but it became vacant after the battle of the Somme. The old man’s son was killed, the mother had already passed away and the old man has gone to live with a daughter. He is pleased that it’s going to a soldier.’ Running along the bottom of the garden is an alley with access to the row of houses, beyond that is open fields. ‘This is more than I expected, dear.’ Harry gives Beryl a fond peck on the cheek.

Harry spins round and announces in an exaggerated fashion ‘Do you think it is grand enough for us to invite the Hemmings over, mother dear?’

‘It damn well will be when I’ve finished with it.’

The weather is mild as they leave their soon-to-be ‘new’ house and continue their journey out of town, walking the two miles to the Hemmings’ house. It is afternoon and Moira Hemmings will be back from church. The Coopers walk up the pebble-crunching drive to the imposing door, at the side of which hangs the cast-iron door bell. They are greeted by Gordon who is pleased to see them both, and in particular to see Harry home from the Front, seemingly in one piece – at least physically.

The hallway to the Hemmings house is as large as the Cooper’s new living room. On the one side stands the grandfather clock and hat stand, on the opposite is a settle with cushions, above it on the wall hangs a large framed photograph; it appears to be of Moira's family. Engravings and pictures – one of which is of a merchant ship, presumably the one in which Gordon served, also hang from the dado rail. The Coopers are ushered through to the conservatory and offered seats on the wicker chairs and settee. In one corner stands an ornate glazed flower pot containing an enormous aspidistra, and scattered in corners in various sized glazed ceramics are Lemon Buttoned Ferns. Beryl is so relieved that her family have moved up a notch on the housing scale. Moira calls for tea.

Moira is keen to talk about the forthcoming wedding, whenever it will be. Conversation, once polite pleasantries are over, turns to James and Susan's future. Where will they live? That is prior to the ending of the war. The Coopers can accommodate them now; however, the obvious place for them to reside is the Hemmings' house, a point made by Moira. 'Aren't we jumping the gun? If you'll pardon the pun – the decision should be theirs,' says Harry. Gordon, the experienced negotiator, whilst agreeing with his wife also concurs with Harry. Not wishing to start a possible disagreement Gordon suggests that the decision be left until the couple come home, adding, 'after all, it is their future.'

Gordon readily agrees to lend Harry one of the firm's trucks for a few hours. That agreed, and with Charlie being given the afternoon off to help them move, they conclude with more polite conversation, before the Coopers leave. On the way out Harry shakes Gordon strongly by the hand. 'Thanks for everything; I've just inspected our new abode'.

'Don't mention it. You deserve it. I particularly wanted to help young Charlie'.

So, with the additional help of Charlie and Harry the furniture is transported from the old to the new house. In truth it doesn't take long as the Coopers have few goods and chattels in their two up, two down old terrace abode.

The few days Harry spends moving house could not have come at a better time. The recommended treatment for shell-shock and designated minor cases is rest, sleep and diversionary activity. The nightmares do not disappear altogether, but diminish in intensity. Beryl resolves to talk to Susan about her father's condition when she comes home; after all, her daughter has more experience in dealing with men suffering from the stresses of war.

She does not have to wait long as Susan arrives home two days later. The joy of family reunion is unbounding. Harry and Beryl are so happy to see their daughter, and Charlie's reserve dissipates at the sight of Susan. In confidence to Susan, Beryl whispers 'If I'm not mistaken, young adolescent Charlie is a little in love with you. Has he met James?'

'No, but he knows all about him.'

‘Ok, but don’t be hugging Charlie too much.’

No. I won’t.

‘I suppose part of the problem is he hardly ever meets other boys. The only people he talks to are older men and women. What can we do? He needs to worry about someone else other than himself…‘I’ve got an idea’ says Beryl. I’ll get Harry to talk to him about a young boy he told me about called Tim. He’s under age and in his platoon. He shouldn’t be in the Army but he has no parents.’

‘Good idea mum, get Charlie to send him a Christmas card and let him know he’s not forgotten, and if he gets a response it will help him realise that he’s not the only one without a mum and dad.’

‘Right, now let’s have another cup of tea and you can tell me about your meeting with James.’

Susan tells her parents of the romantic tryst. She keeps no secrets from them, she knows they understand how she feels and, given their history, would not feel justified in disapproving. When visiting the Hemmings her story is curtailed, being devoid of the more romantic parts of the event. But of course, Gordon and Moira are more than pleased to know first-hand that their son is alive and well.

At the Coopers' new house there is much scrubbing, painting, hanging of curtains and purchasing of some furniture; luckily the previous occupants left a considerable amount by way of armchairs, a settee and a dining room suite. The Coopers settle into their new home with ease, Susan and Charlie are particularly pleased at having their own bedrooms.

During a quiet moment when Susan and Beryl are alone the question of Harry's nightmares is discussed. Susan is disturbed at hearing of her father's problem but assures her mother that it doesn't appear to be overly serious. Susan has served for a while in a psychiatric ward and has seen much worse cases, who, she assures her mother, do eventually recover.

'But I've heard that they brand anyone suffering in this way as a coward. Your father is no coward. They wouldn't have promoted him if he was.'

'Attitudes have changed mum. That's what they thought three years ago in 1914. Now they're more sympathetic. They have hospitals especially for the worst cases.'

'How bad is your dad? Will he have to go to hospital or will they shove him straight back in the firing line?'

'Unless he displays symptoms of instability in front of the men, he will be returned to duty.'

‘God, you make it sound like a military instruction. You haven’t seen or heard him shouting for help, he hasn’t cried in your arms. He’s not completely well.’

‘I’m sorry mum, but that is how it is. Until there’s a complete breakdown and he’s seen not to function as an effective soldier, this is what they’ll do.’

‘I’m worried Susan even though he has improved since he’s been at home. Moving house and beginning the decoration has been a sort of treatment, but I fear more bad experiences in the trenches could tip him over the edge.’

There is nothing either of the women can do but keep an eye on him for the remaining few days of leave that he has left, and then hope to God he survives both physically and mentally when he returns to the firing line.

The all-too-brief leave passes and Harry is preparing to go back to the war.

Come the day of departure Harry is escorted by Beryl, Susan and Charlie. They walk to the station. Charlie insists on carrying Harry’s rifle. Each succeeding good-bye engenders a greater feeling of emotion as if the odds of returning are getting less and less. Beryl is mightily concerned about Harry’s emotional fitness. The last night at home was disturbing as neither could sleep. Beryl held him tight and would not let go. 'Don't worry dear, I'll be back. If I've lasted this long; I must be a survivor,' he says. Beryl is not convinced.

Susan is more sanguine, and perversely hopes that he might suffer a minor breakdown. Her reasoning being that he could then be taken out of the line and possibly sent back to Blighty. This optimistic view is, she confesses, a long-shot.

To Charlie, his uncle Harry has become a bit of a hero. When he chose to talk about the trenches he did not shirk from providing the boy with an up-to-date picture, albeit with the more gory details being omitted. In a move of affection Harry ruffles Charlie's hair and reminds him to send a card to Private Tim. 'And remember what your aunt Beryl told you' he says with some solemnity 'you have a family, he hasn't.' Charlie promises to comply with this request.

On the last night of his leave Harry stands in their new garden with Beryl. 'I look forward to decorating more of this place; I might even put up a small shed in the garden.'

'Well, I'll have to give the house a good scrubbing first. It still smells a bit musty,' comments Beryl as she looks upwards at the brightly shining moon. 'You know Harry I like looking at the moon.'

‘Oh, why’s that then; you’re not getting over romantic in your old age, are you?’ jokes Harry.

‘I don’t know what it’s like at the Front; I can’t share that with you and you can’t share what it’s like over here, but at night we’re both looking at the same moon: it’s something we can both share at the same time; I like that Harry, it makes me feel a bit closer to you.’

On the following morning the train shunts into the station and with a loud hiss of steam, and screeching of brakes it grinds to a halt. Susan and Beryl cannot hide their emotions. Charlie, having tried to shake Harry’s hand in a strong manly manner, moves away in order to try and conceal the tears welling up in his eyes.

The train is packed with returning soldiers; a few are from the East Kent Regiment. There are brief ‘Hallos’ as Harry boards the train. Like all departing troops he then remains hanging out of the carriage window waving vigorously until his family disappear out of sight.

It is a quiet, tearful and forlorn group that wends its way back to the house.

CHAPTER TWENTY-NINE

The journey back to France is uneventful. The ship is crammed full of returning soldiers with one regiment of 'red arses', i.e. battle virgins. The latter sit around the deck saying not very much. In truth they are a little in awe of the returning experienced combatants: after a year or more on the Front line the latter can be regarded as veterans. The inexperienced troops are not ignored by the 'old hands', rather, like the civilians at home, they haven't much to contribute to the conversation. This is not to say that the returnees are particularly overjoyed about going back to the battlefront, but what they do have is shared experiences which act as a kind of corporate bonding; to the outsider it appears as a barrier. Their stories, their jokes, their comradeship cannot, as yet, be fully shared.

It is not until the ship docks and Harry is ushered onto the train heading for Etaples that he bumps into some close old friends. He is hoping to meet his long-time colleague and pal Lieutenant Boneaply; they have now served in the same unit for over two years.

Harry and the other occupants of the carriage fall silent as they listen to the engine puff and then hiss, spitting out steam as if in disgust at being back at the terminus; the locomotive seems not too keen to get nearer to the Front. Is this the gateway to hell, muses Harry. Most of the soldiers are not, understandably, looking forward to going back to the discomfort of trench life; some, however, now feel totally out of place in the civilian environment, although the thought of being 'beasted' again over the sand dunes in the 'Bull Ring' by sadistic instructors in Etaples does not inspire joy. They are informed on their arrival that, being experienced soldiers, their stay in Etaples will only last a couple of days; this is a relief – not having to carrying full kit and running over the sand dunes is a blessed relief. Time is spent on the shooting ranges and, where necessary, exchanging unserviceable kit and uniforms.

Harry and Boney meet up on the ranges and at the conclusion of a shooting detail they walk to the YMCA canteen. They enjoy their chats. They have become confidants even though Boney is now a commissioned officer. But they are different in that Boney is a professional soldier whose life is the Army. He's not married and when on leave he stays with a relative.

'How did your leave go, Boney?'

'Quiet. I stay with my "skin n'blister"' says Boney reverting to his cockney rhyming-slang. 'She lives in Rochester, she's a nice old girl but we don't have much in common. Once we've reminisced about the family and I've done the heavy chores, there's nothing much left to talk about. The people in the pub, as you know, haven't a bloody clue. In truth I miss the banter with the blokes out here – bloody sad! What about you? Weren't you moving house?'

'Yeah, I spent most of my leave working on the new house. It was very helpful exercise and not just in a practical way: it took my mind off the war. I have to confess to you Boney that I'm getting awful nightmares. It's upsetting. My missus is worried that I might crack when I'm at the Front.'

'What you need Harry is a complete rest for a few weeks, not just a few days. Very occasionally they send experienced people back to the depot in Blighty for a spell, to act as instructors. If I hear of anything happening in that direction I'll let you know.'

'Thanks Boney. In the meantime we've got the problem of fighting a 'little' war. What's the state of play, do you know?'

'Don't know the details of course, but we – along with the Canadians and Australians – will be advancing over a broad front. Secrecy is the name of the game we're told. So, no early bombardment of the enemy, but we will have a lot of tanks. I guess they'll use them as a surprise.'

'I hope the top brass know what they're doing. Where do they get their info from?'

‘Much of it comes from photos taken by the fly boys with their cameras. Isn’t your future son-in-law one of them?’

‘Yeah, he is. He and Susan are to be married on his next leave which is due about now – although I expect it will be postponed until after this next push.’

‘What about you, Boney? You should be due for retirement, once this ruddy war is over.’

‘I was … I am … but there’s no chance of it happening at the moment.’

‘Sounds like this next push will be a big one. We’ve got to be winning. I’ve heard they’re sending over more of the reserve battalions from England and more and more Yanks are arriving. We must outnumber the Hun by now.’

‘We’ll soon find out the score. We’re off up the Line later this afternoon,’ concludes Lieutenant Boneaply.

‘Take care Boney, I want to see you at my daughter’s wedding in the not too distant future, Cheerio old son’.

Two days more and the regiment is ensconced in a trench awaiting instructions. A runner came round with watches at 0400, they had already been synchronised. It is now 0500 hours. There is a deep chill in the air; men are shivering with cold and dreaded anticipation of what is to come. The company commander is looking at his watch and is holding his whistle to his lips. The troops are nervously awaiting the order to go over the top. The weather is on the side of the allies as the shell pitted fields of Picardy are covered in a dense blanket of fog, reminiscent of the raw sea-mist that often pervades the coast of East Kent: this should help the planned-for surprise assault.

Looking along the trench Harry can see the young lad who he had first noticed in a tunnel prior to an attack last year. It's Tim Gibson and he's still under the legal age for combat. He remembers that the lad held it together following the Arras battle. There is a mistaken belief that the longer in combat the greater the confidence and the more capable a soldier is at handling the stress: not true, of course, as Harry knows. Practically speaking the soldier is more efficient but this constant battering of the senses, particularly the nerves, can have a detrimental effect. Harry takes a closer look at young Tim and notices he is nearing the point of paralysis; alarmingly, his hands are shaking and he's fumbling with his kit and can't secure the bayonet on his rifle. Shellshock affects soldiers in different ways. The lad ought to come out of the line but there is no way this can be allowed to happen, certainly not at this late hour. Harry moves across, puts a hand on Gibson's shoulder and taking the rifle from him, fixes the bayonet on the end. No words are spoken: just a terrified look from Private Gibson and a kindly grimace from his Sergeant-major.

Moving back to his vantage point Harry is conscious of someone vomiting. Others praying, some cross themselves but most just stand there with a resigned stare, waiting for the inevitable sign which could signal the end of life, at least as they know it.

The British artillery opens-up, and a hail of metal flies overhead. During a very brief lull in the barrage the clarion call is heard, ‘Steady the Buffs’. The heralding of the regimental motto acts as a rallying cry and men’s backs stiffen. Its collective significance is not lost.

All along the line men from three continents are poised. To the north are the British supported by parts of an American division. Across the river and to the south are the Australians and Canadians. Then the French bombardment heralds the start of the battle, supported by the British guns. Following the initial attack the French troop’s advance; later to be supported by tanks.

The noise, as it always is on a battle field, is deafening. The advantage of the dense fog, now beginning to rise, is apparent as the troops pick their way across no-man’s land. The element of surprise works as the enemy’s response is delayed initially, and is therefore less effective. Within three hours the first objective has been taken. Much of the dreaded hand-to-hand fighting does not happen as the enemy is surrendering in substantial numbers. Any retaliation from the retreating Germans is ineffective as they are being attacked constantly by British planes, one of which is flown by Lieutenant James Hemmings.

Harry looks skywards and raised his rifle in salute to James and his comrades. The allies push on, and by the end of the fourth day after spasmodic fighting the British troops have advanced into enemy territory.

The battle is not over. Harry and his company are ordered to consolidate their position; in doing so they explore the captured redoubt and extensive German trench system. The strength and depth of their fortifications astonishes Harry. Rummaging through the underground catacomb-like cells Harry and some of his companions are struck by the obvious panic that must have ensued, evidenced by the personal details that the enemy hurriedly discarded. Apart from the obvious detritus of war, the guns and the ammunition, the exodus must have been so hurried that intimate effects are left; photographs of families, of children and letters. On occasions like this the soldier is reminded that his enemy is also human and the futility of war strikes home. Harry, more than ever, wants to be back with his family.

Company officers and Company Sergeant-major Cooper are summoned by Colonel Howard-Bains, the commanding officer, for the post-combat briefing. The Colonel taps the bowl of his pipe in a confident manner: 'the day appears to have gone well,' he says before imparting what news he has gleaned from talking to the Brigadier and other visiting staff officers. Addressing the ensemble he coughs, clears his throat and, as if delivering a political speech, makes his pronouncement:

'This latest battle for Amiens has been a turning point and the enemy is now on the defensive and many thousands of prisoners have been taken. I congratulate you all for the stern and courageous effort you and your soldiers have shown; please convey this to your companies. I know this has been achieved with a considerable number of casualties, so do ensure that all serious cases are effectively and speedily transferred A.S.A.P to the clearing stations for necessary medical treatment. This offensive is to be discontinued in this sector, but it is not over; time must now be spent re-arming and consolidating our newly won position. Above our heads the aviators are still at it. Well done to you all.'

This news is, naturally, a great relief. The chances are that the regiment will soon be relieved by the reserve battalion.

Harry and Boney take the opportunity to have a brief chat on the way back to company HQ. On arrival, having posted sentries they obtain a brew and sit on the fire step. The weather has changed and it is now a barmy summer evening and there is no evidence of the ubiquitous heavy mist of the previous days. Boney lights his pipe, leans back against the slatted wall of the trench and puffs out the grey-blue smoke which spirals upwards like the remnants from a smouldering bombed-out building. Harry lights a cigarette.

'If what I hear is true about more reserve battalions being posted out here from Blighty, and more and more Yanks now in the Line, I wouldn't be surprised if we are one of the units to go home. After all, I think we've done enough,' comments Boney.

Harry, in a more reflective mood, answers in a plaintive manner, 'I think those who are dead are the ones who've done enough.'

A few planes are still zig-zagging across the sky. They had witnessed one bi-plane limp over their new position before diving into a shell hole. Fortunately it was a Hun. On reaching the wreckage the first priority is retrieving the camera and then the pilot. The aviators are expendable compared to expensive equipment, particularly the enemy's maps.

CHAPTER THIRTY

The airmen see the battle from a different perspective. On the battle field the infantry commander, via his signallers, assures the pilots that the mist had cleared enough for the squadron to prepare to get airborne. The foot soldiers and, in particular the gunners, require more precise target information, which The Royal Flying Corps provides.

The battle over Amiens has now been raging for several days and below, stretching over a wide front, the infantry are seen scattered over the countryside like strewn-out lines of hurrying ants. Ahead are the British tanks. Grey-clad figures can be detected emerging from the German trenches, many of them scurrying rearward in an attempt to escape from the oncoming slaughter. The superior number of allied troops is obvious from the air.

The pilots test their guns and continue over their own lines, and head toward the enemy's heavy guns. The objective is to silence them or at least ensure that the enemy keeps his head down, thus restricting any effective retaliation.

Seeing the troops below James spares a momentary thought for his future father-in-law. He hopes Harry will survive this encounter and recalls telling him when last they met, that he would never want to exchange places. It is dangerous in the air but at least there is the opportunity to try and outfox your opponent, and when the situation becomes too tricky, there's the chance to escape. The thought of Harry reminds him of Susan. Just another week or so before this 'little fracas' is over and he'll be back home and walking down the aisle.

The diversionary thoughts are rudely interrupted when the silhouette of German Fokkers come out of the sun and into view. James' squadron leader fires the opening shot and dives, the remainder follow suit. The enemy breaks formation and engages on an individual basis. A dog-fight begins. The air is full of whirling, twisting machines spitting bullets. It's each man for himself. James faces a Fokker head on. He presses the trigger and dives and swerves off just in time. He hears rounds go zip, zip over his left shoulder; more side-slipping and dodging with short bursts from machine guns.

James is alone. The dog-fight had ended almost as soon as it began. An enemy bi-plane is careering towards the earth. Attempts now have to be made to reform the V formation, but there is no friendly aircraft in sight. When isolated it is best to give it full throttle; assume that the others have either been downed or are heading back in order to re-arm; it's therefore full speed and head for home.

James cranes his neck left and right to check the enemy's not on his tail. He sees nothing but the red streaks of tracer rounds criss-crossing the air. Blackish clouds of explosive anti-aircraft fire litter the air space; clearly enemy fire is getting denser, hastening his desire to escape.

Hun aircraft have disappeared but now the concern is the stream of thick oily smoke following James' aeroplane. Another look over his shoulder and the problem becomes clear, or rather not clear as the atmosphere is blackened with oil that is spewing out of a fuel pipe. Rounds from a chasing Fokker must have split the pipe and now the engine vibrates while the revolution-counter indicates a rapid decrease in speed.

The British lines are twelve miles away. There is nothing James can do. He keeps an eye on the altimeter, and prays. The ultimate objective is getting nearer but so is the ground … fifteen thousand feet … ten thousand feet and falling. James has landed before with wings shredded with bullet holes, but then the engine was still functioning. If the engine seizes up altogether then the end, for the aircraft and him, could come very quickly.

The engine begins to cough and splutter as he nears the British trenches. To say that the flight is now turbulent, chaotic even, is an understatement. Although still a few hundred feet above the trench, the British soldiers instinctively duck as the plane careers overhead just before the motor cuts out altogether. The only sound now is from the air humming through the struts, the broken wires supporting the wings. James switches off the engine, not that this makes any difference. He braces himself against impact as the plane drifts across the uneven shell holes of the fought over battlefield. Gliding into wind helps slow the aircraft down but it doesn't prevent a dipping wing tip hitting a protruding edge of a bomb crafter. Balance interrupted means the plane somersaults, flips over so it lands on the ground upside down. The propeller buries itself in the earth; the fuselage is sticking vertically upwards: another mangled piece of wreckage soon to be added to the detritus of war.

Beneath this pile of metal, wood and wires is a human being. The roundels, identifiable two hundred yards away, indicate to the observers that it is one of ours.

Soldiers in the trenches are transfixed. They continue to stare at the aircraft as if having just witnessed a high flying trapeze act that went drastically wrong.

'Jesus Christ, did you bloody see that!' exclaims one.

'Gibson, Wild, Collins, Willoughby' shouts the Sergeant-major. 'Two of you grab that stretcher and follow me: at the double!' He snatches up a first aid kit and charges across the pitted Picardy landscape in an effort to rescue the unfortunate pilot. The wreckage is lying just short of the previously occupied trenches. Oil is splattered all around. It is essential to get the pilot clear in case the whole thing goes up in smoke, as they frequently do on impact.

The pilot is half hanging out of the cockpit.

The leader of the rescue party circles round looking for an attached camera while the soldiers lift the airman free from the aircraft. The headquarter staff always ask for the camera first; they want evidence of enemy positions, armaments, of troop movements. Pilots come second. There is no camera.

The flyer is laid carefully face down. 'Right, turn him over … careful now,' instructs Sergeant-major Cooper. The flying helmet has slid down over the pilot's face, He removes it gingerly. Harry stands up abruptly. He is shocked. 'James, James … Are you OK?' Silly question! He clearly isn't. Blood seeps out of the side of his mouth. Harry does a head to toe check. James has no feeling in his legs; as a precaution Harry straps the legs together. 'We'll get you to the first aid post as quick as we can,' he says in earnest.

'Do you know him sir?' inquires Willoughby.

'Yes.'

'Harry, thank God it's you,' splutters James.

‘Don’t speak, James. Save your energy. Right … lads … gently … now. We’re going to lift you onto the stretcher, James.’ As gingerly as they can they place James on to the conveyance and position themselves at each corner. Gripping the wooden handles, the stretcher is raised. They walk as carefully as they can over the uneven ground. It means circumnavigating the shell holes. Meanwhile James is slipping in and out of consciousness.

They go down the communication trench and out onto the nearby road. ‘Is he a relative sir?’ asks Gibson.

‘He hopes to be my son-in-law soon.’

‘Do you think he’ll make it sir,’ asks another.

‘God, I bloody hope so!’

Fortuitously a truck is passing. It’s flagged down. The casualty is loaded onto the back. The lads are sent back to report to the company commander and told to explain why he, Sergeant-major Cooper, has stayed with the injured pilot and gone to the first-aid clearing station.

Gibson, the youngest but the senior of the four soldiers reports to the company commander who is in conversation with Lieutenant Boneaply. ‘Did Mr Cooper address the pilot as James?’ enquires Lieutenant Boneaply.

‘Yes, sir, that’s what he called him.’

‘Poor bastard.’ exclaims Lieutenant Boneaply sadly. He then explains why the CSM has to stay with the casualty. Once Private Gibson is thanked and dismissed the two officers discuss Harry Cooper. Quite apart from the people they have all seen maimed or killed, the fact that two of them are Harry’s family members, and that he is experiencing nightmares is a concern. ‘This suggests,’ says Lieutenant Boneaply, ‘that he could be nearing breaking point.’

‘It wouldn’t do for the men to see our stoic, seasoned veteran and dependable Sergeant-major cracking up,’ concludes the company commander. ‘There is, I hear, an outsize possibility in the near future, of the battalion being exchanged for one presently stationed in Blighty. If, and when that is the case Sergeant-major Cooper can join the advance party, so we can get him back home as soon as possible: but I wouldn’t bet on it, so don’t get your or his hopes up.’ There is a great concern for Harry Cooper, he is part of the backbone of the company, and he’s seen more action than most; he and Lieutenant Boneaply are the longest serving members of the outfit.

‘Keep going James. I’ll wait here for you.’ Harry squeezes James’ hand; he feels a faint response. James, on reaching the medical clearing station, is carried straight into the temporary surgery.

Meanwhile Harry sits in the bench waiting on the doctor's assessment and prognosis. An orderly provides him with a welcome mug of tea. Harry leans back against the tented support and closes his eyes. He tries to keep awake but the drama of the past few days overcomes his resistance. He wakes when, after some considerable time, the doctor comes into the outer tent.

He sees Harry sitting there. 'Are you alright Sergeant-major Cooper?'

'How's the patient?'

'I can't quite understand why you're so concerned about a young officer in a different unit? Are you related, or what?

'Almost.'

'What do you mean, almost?'

'He's due to be my son-in-law when he gets home in a week or two, unless he has to spend some time in hospital.'

'Oh! I see. I'm afraid he won't be going home in a week or two … and he won't be going to the hospital … in fact, he won't be going anywhere … I'm sorry.'

Harry’s reaction is stark and immediate; choking back the tears, he buries his head in his hands. Once again he feels that all too familiar hurt, the sickening clench in the pit of his stomach.

The doctor disappears only to re-appear a few moments later. In one hand he has a photograph and in the other, two letters.

‘What’s your daughter’s name?’

‘Susan … Susan Cooper.’

The doctor turns the photo over, the inscription reads ‘*To Darling James, all my love Susan*’.

He then hands the photo and the letters to Harry. ‘I think you had better have these. Here’s a photo and two letters ready for posting to your Susan.’ The medical officer disappears straight away only to come back shortly. ‘I think your daughter might like to have these as well.’ With the other hand he gives Harry the flier’s emblem – his wings badge – and his flying helmet with goggles. The doctor had thoughtfully detached the badge from James’s tunic.

‘I’ll keep the other means of identification and pass them on to his commanding officer,’ adds the medical officer.

'Yes, of course, I'd best get back to my unit now … thanks.' With that Harry departs. He is offered a lift part of the way but shuns the offer, preferring to walk back and gather his thoughts. He allows his emotions to be released on his private walk to his lines; tears stream down his cheeks. He is most concerned for Susan. Someone will have to inform her. The Army won't. James's commanding officer will naturally write to Gordon and Moira: he will have to break the terrible news to Susan.

The land across to Amiens has been secured and all is now quiet on this section of the Western Front. An hour later, oblivious to the rain that is now falling and churning up the topography of the battlefield, Harry arrives back at his company headquarters. The company commander and Lieutenant 'Boney' are there to greet him.

They don't need to ask him what the outcome is: it's written all over his tired face and abundantly evident by his red and bleary eyes. The major calls for the orderly and instructs him to rustle up something to eat for Harry, while Boney fills his cup adding a generous shot of rum.

'Someone has to tell my Susan, his fiancée, about this. It will have to be me. I'm not used to writing obituaries,' moans Harry.

‘I’ll give you a hand,’ says the company commander. ‘But I suggest you leave it for a while. You don’t want your daughter to hear the bad news before the deceased’s parents are informed. If they inform her, OK, but not the other way round. That wouldn’t help at all. I’d wait until his unit OC has had the chance to contact his next of kin.’

CHAPTER THIRTY-ONE

It is a September morning and the signs of summer remain detectable; many of the plants are still flowering while others are beginning to wilt, and some of the leaves are providing evidence of the coming autumn. Despite this the Kent countryside looks a picture.

Gordon and Moira Hemmings have made a list, in conjunction with Susan Cooper, of the requirements for the forthcoming planned wedding. The banns have been read and the restaurant has been booked for the reception; the hotel where the two families first met was jointly agreed and selected as the most convenient and appropriate venue; it is decided that it won’t be a lavish affair due to the uncertainty of wartime arrangements.

Gordon has completed a War Department interim report before going to the Gunpowder factory, so he is still at home when the post arrives.

Due to his occupation it is not unusual to received correspondence in buff envelopes. While sifting through the mail Moira inquires if he wants another cup of coffee, before going into the kitchen. As she vacates the dining room, she calls, 'Let me know if there is anything from James.'

The last envelope lay on the table. It is smaller than the others and does not have the imprint of a London post mark: he realises with some concern that it is a private War Office stamped communique. He slides the paper knife under the flap and reads. His blood turns cold. The stab to the heart releases a cry from deep down inside him. 'Oh, No. No. No. Oh … God!' Moira unused to hearing her urbane husband react to anything in such a dramatic way, dashes into the dining room. Gordon is bent forward his head in his hands with tears of grief welling in his eyes. 'What does it say?' She exclaims. With a trembling hand Gordon holds the letter at arms-length. Half guessing, half knowing she accepts the letter, not wanting but of necessity having to read it. It is addressed to both of them:

Dear Sir and Madam,

We have been engaged in a decisive battle on the North Western Front. As ordered James's squadron took to the air. The tanks and the infantry had advanced into enemy territory and it was our job to aid them by ensuring we kept the enemy guns as silent as possible. The task was almost complete when on our way back to HQ we encountered a squadron of enemy fighters. James, as expected, excelled himself and downed one of their aircraft, but in doing so his aeroplane suffered damage and oil could be seen streaming from his engine. He had no alternative but to head straight for home. Losing height and clearly in trouble he had the sense to maintain direction and the skill to keep his aircraft from colliding with our soldiers in the trenches. James and his aircraft sustained considerable damage on impact with the ground behind our lines. A section of infantry led by Warrant Officer Cooper went to his aid and transported him to the nearest first aid post. The medics did their best but alas, James did not survive the ordeal. His passing will receive due honour and respect at the military funeral that will take place in the morning.

I do hope that I have not caused you more pain than is necessary in passing on these details, but assumed you would want to know soonest. I am assured that Mr Cooper will be in touch with you when he comes home; he is writing to

James' fiancée, whom I'm informed is his daughter.

I must say that your son James was an exceptional pilot and first-rate RFC officer, and that he was an immensely popular member of the squadron, and will be forever missed. To say that he was a credit to the squadron, and in particular to you, is an understatement. Our heartfelt sympathy goes to you and your family.
Yours truly,
Major R Pendleton MC RFC
Squadron Commander

Moira becomes hysterically inconsolable; beating Gordon about the chest while wailing her hurt by uncontrollably screaming her son's name. The rest of her day is viewed through a vail of lachrymose rage. She cannot rest, cannot sit, cannot be still, cannot eat or drink; it will be hours before she gains a sense of control: followed by a lifetime of pain.

Later in the day Gordon makes a brief visit to the factory. He is seen lowering the Union Jack flag to half-mast. There is no need to explain to the employees who is the latest victim of the war. Thc loss is felt throughout the firm, James was very popular: and they were all looking forward to his forthcoming wedding.

Gordon and Moira's residence was not the only house to be drawing their curtains due to loss and bereavement. Although James was not yet a member of their household, Beryl also closes their drapes.

Susan is heard howling in despair and will not leave her room. The only person who can lend a consoling hand is Charlie. His arms encircle her as he utters, 'I know how yer feel.' And he too sobs.

Sharing Susan's grief acts as a valve of release for Charlie, until then unable to completely let go and release his emotions. Susan has become more of a sister than a cousin and he shares her loss and in doing so, at long last, feels permitted to publically express his own sorrow.

CHAPTER THIRTY-TWO

Harry returns to his unit which is ensconced in the recently acquired German trench. The Tommies are amazed at the strength of the German fortifications, which are deeper and more solid than the British and Allies entrenchment. Personal souvenirs are collected; helmets, bayonets, anything with a regimental badge. Sentries are detailed to take post, others are sent out to no-man's-land to help with the wounded. Some take the opportunity to rest, to sleep.

Morale is good. News has filtered down that the Canadians and Australians have secured more ground. The sun is beginning to descend over the horizon while the French artillery intermittently carry-on bombarding the enemy six miles to the West. Senses are being relaxed as adrenalin levels subside and fatigue starts to set in. Few notice the seeping, creeping low cloud of yellow-green vapour advancing imperceptibly across the battle field. It is heading towards those concentrating on collecting the wounded; out there leading the operation is Sergeant-major Harry Cooper.

A frantic voice is heard screaming: 'Gas! Gas! Gas!' The evening breeze carrying the pungent, nauseating, foul-tasting vapour scorches the throat and sears the eyes of Harry, and his working party. The gas bomb fortunately clears the crowded trench but those in the pitted earth of the killing-field are falling like playing cards in a collapsing pack.

As the bilious cloud rolls onward in an easterly direction, those in the trench scramble to don gas masks and get ready to rescue their comrades. Tim Gibson peers above the parapet and spots the Sergeant-major; without waiting for an order he scales the ladder, dashes across the mangled waste to Harry Cooper. His action is instinctive; he remembers his Sergeant-major comforting him; this is his chance to repay Harry's concern.

Harry Cooper is on his knees, gasping for air, choking, half-vomiting when Gibson arrives.

'I'm here, sir, I'm here … let me help you.' He wrestles Harry's gasmask out of its holder; thrusts it over his face; secures the straps; ducks under Harry's left arm and throws it across his own shoulders. Harry strains, grips his rifle barrel in his right hand, with the butt on the ground he uses it as a prop. 'Come on sir, you can make it,' Tim Gibson tries to shout; words getting muffled under his respirator. They are struggling to stand upright. The Sergeant-major now reliant on the Private is bent in half; knees buckle; gasmask is lifted to expectorate phlegm. Progress is slow as Private Gibson drags his mentor and leader back towards the trench.

One eye is closed the other is squinting through a slit; it opens enough for Harry to recognise his rescuer. Amid coughs and splutters Harry reaches up from a stretcher and grips Gibson's arm; 'Thank you Tim lad' he splutters. Tim Gibson watches as they carry the injured sergeant-major away to the Casualty Clearing Station. Inwardly he feels pleased, gratified, that he has been able to help the man who cared about him.

Harry is not enjoying the rickety ambulance drive, but is happier when he is off-loaded into the ward at Le Trèport hospital. He's dirty, smelly and sweaty, throat is raw, eyes still streaming and lids are swollen and, according to a nursing sister his temperature is high. He's not as bad as some, those exposed for longer are dangerously ill: thank God for Private Gibson. Harry resolves to write to him once he has fully recovered.

A fortnight has passed and several of the worse cases have died from gas induced bronchitis. Harry is still wheezing and coughing but improving. 'Am I going back up the line?' He enquires of the newly arrived sister.

'What's your name, m'dear?' she asks as she picks up the clipboard.

'I know you, don't I?' he rasps.

'You're a bit quick to try it on, we've only just met, m'dear.'

'No, no', he says between gulps of air. 'My daughter told me about you.'

Nurse Doris looks again at the name on the clipboard.

'Cooper, Sergeant-major Harry Cooper … not Susan's dad?' she exclaims joyfully. 'Is she married yet, m'dear?'

There is a longish pause. Doris is not sure if it's because of his injury, but then observes the contortioned look and welling puffiness of his eyes.

‘Oh, she’s not … been hurt, m’dear has she?’

‘Not physically’, he gasps. ‘No.’

‘Is it James … is he …?’

Harry clutches his throat and nods.

‘Oh! Dear. Dear.’ After a few moments Nurse Doris composes herself and asks ‘Does she know you’re here, m’dear.’

Between a coughing bout Harry looks at the sister and makes a sign as if to write.

‘Of course, m’dear; I’ll write to her. I’ll do it tonight. I’ll let her know you’ll be coming home.’

A further two weeks pass before Harry Cooper is deemed able to be transported by ambulance and train to the harbour at Boulogne, and then on a troop ship back to Folkestone. No more the acrid smell of gas, gangrene, pus and antiseptics. It means, home and a spell in a convalescent hospital before seeing the family again. Beryl makes a couple of trips to the hospital, this aids his recovery.

CHAPTER THIRTY-THREE

Susan has received Doris's letter and so they are all waiting anxiously for Harry's return. When he arrives he wastes no time in acquainting the Hemmings family with the painful circumstances witnessed during James's last moments. He also returns Susan's letters along with the pilot's flying 'wings' and flying helmet.

Harry has been told that in order to aid his recovery he should exercise, and Beryl has got used to Harry's 'evening strolls' as she calls them. It is at this time of the day particularly, when Harry's thoughts return to the trenches in France and Belgium. It is when walking through the town towards the coast that the cooling effect of the sea mist and on-shore breezes act as refreshment initially; but this it is also when, during these quiet, reflective moments when the sun dips below the horizon, that senses are jerked into life, and echoes of the past events are seen and heard; like cinematic images, they pass before his eyes. The light is beginning to fade and the spotlight of war in the shape of the moon rises to reveal each vivid icon of memory. It is the time of day when he can, with impunity, release his inner emotions without suffering the indignity of interruption or feelings of embarrassment. 'It takes time to readjust,' he tells Beryl. 'It's been nearly four years of killing and dying, and I'm ruddy well tired out.'

In truth, Beryl thinks he will never be fully fit again, either mentally or physically. Decorating the house and digging the garden help the physical rejuvenation but it is the walking, the thinking and the grieving that is most necessary.

Beryl, Charlie and Susan are also still in an emotional turmoil. Susan finds it increasingly hard to sleep and is prone to moments of weeping. Not seeing James's final resting place is emotionally upsetting for both her and his parents. Beryl is worried about her daughter; physically she appears fine but nevertheless her concern is such that she suggests that Susan talks to one of the doctors.

The local vicar, aware of the plight afflicting the Hemmings and the Coopers proposes to hold a memorial service for the benefit of the families particularly, but also for friends and relatives. Harry now feels capable of attending such a commemoration; it is to be held in a fortnight's time on a Friday evening at the local parish church.

On the morning of the service Susan has to disappear to visit the hospital. 'Do you have to go this morning?' enquires Harry.

'It's alright dad I won't be long; I just need a check-up.'

I'll be back in plenty of time for church this evening.

‘Well, mind you are. This is one parade you don’t want to be late for.’

The two families meet at the guildhall in Faversham before proceeding together to the church. The church is said to be the second largest in the county; they wait outside, stare at the gravestones, read the scrolls and carved headstones: that James’s name will not be immortalised is lamented. Gordon promises that one day there will be a memorial in the church with James’s name inscribed upon it.

The congregation rises when the vicar, followed by the Hemmings and the Coopers take their places in the front pews. The remainder of the church is filled with friends, relatives, and workers from the gunpowder factory. There is also a contingent from the East Kent Regiment, which has by this time returned to England. Near the front of the church is the recently promoted Captain Boneaply, and next to him is Private Tim Gibson who has come especially in order to thank Sergeant-major Cooper for his very kind letter. He also wants to say a heartfelt ‘Thank you’ to Charlie Smith for the thoughtful Christmas and birthday cards: they meant more to him than words can say. Included is a squadron from the flying station at Manston, and a group of nurses; at the rear of the church sits Mr and Mrs Parting alongside Sister Doris.

In the absence of a coffin the vicar has placed a simple wooden chair in front of the altar, over which is draped a

Union Jack and on which rests James' flying helmet, goggles, wings badge and an RFC cap badge. The simplicity of this display is made more poignant when highlighted by a penetrating moonbeam shining through the stain glass window. The gusts of wind rustle the outside branches disturbing the moonlight that illuminates the regimental display: the whole scene appears in motion. The red, white and blue of the flag seeks to quiver, glass goggles reflect the evening light, while the silver RFC and wings badge flicker, glisten and fade in the flare of the white moon beam, mimicking small explosions.

The impressive acoustics ensure the sound of songs reverberate with emotion as feelings are allowed free rein, and there is hardly a dry eye when the congregation give voice to '*There's a Long, Long Trail a Winding'*. The latter was requested by Susan.

On completion of the memorial service and following polite and earnest expressions of sympathy for the families, people drift off home; some make for the station while the uniformed military attendants disperse in an army vehicle. Private Gibson warmly shakes Harry's hand; Harry is greatly touched by the efforts the lad made in contacting him. Tim Gibson makes a point of telling Charlie that he will continue to write to him; a gesture that makes Charlie happy. Prior to his departure Boney seeks out Harry. Harry is pleased to have the opportunity to speak to his old pal and introduce him to his family. 'We feel as if we already know you,' says Beryl before inviting him to visit their home at a later date, an invitation Captain Boneaply readily accepts before departing. Doris hugs Susan before waving a heartfelt good-bye.

Finally, after thanking the vicar and bidding him 'farewell' the Hemmings and Coopers make their way to the Lychgate. They pause, the autumnal air is chilly. The cemetery next to the church is too strident a reminder at this time and they are disinclined to linger; mouthing farewells are awkward at such a moment.

Gordon Hemmings reiterates his offer to Harry about obtaining him a job at the gunpowder factory, but adds 'as the papers say, it may not be too long before this wretched business is completely over, and so I am unsure about the future of the factory. We might both be looking for alternate employment.'

'We'll just have to take it as it comes, Mr Hemmings' says Harry trying to sound hopeful.

Looking back at the church Moira pulls a handkerchief from her coat pocket. Dabbing her eyes again, she exclaims 'The hardest thing isn't just not seeing him; it's not being able to touch, to hold a part of him. Susan embraces her.

A final shake of hands and the two families part company.

Charlie, noticing the seemingly permanent distressed nature of Moira Hemmings says, with due lack of thought pertaining to adolescence, ‘I don’t suppose we’ll be seeing her again too often.’

‘I think we will,’ responds Beryl.

‘Oh, why is that?’ asks Harry looking a little startled.

According to a doctor, I think we could soon be grandparents, announces Beryl’.

Printed in Great Britain
by Amazon

64304391R00173